Agatha Rai...

DEAD ON TARGET

M.C. Beaton

Agatha Raisin

DEAD ON TARGET

with R.W. Green

CONSTABLE

CONSTABLE

First published in Great Britain in 2023 by Constable

Copyright © M. C. Beaton, 2023

M.C. BEATON® and AGATHA RAISIN® are registered
trademarks of M.C. Beaton Limited

1 3 5 7 9 10 8 6 4 2

The moral right of the author has been asserted.

*All characters and events in this publication, other than
those clearly in the public domain, are fictitious
and any resemblance to real persons,
living or dead, is purely coincidental.*

A CIP catalogue record for this book
is available from the British Library.

ISBN 978-1-40871-850-6

Typeset in Palatino by Hewer Text UK Ltd, Edinburgh
Printed and bound in Great Britain by Clays Ltd, Elcograf S.p.A.

Papers used by Constable are from well-managed
forests and other responsible sources

MIX
Supporting
responsible forestry
FSC® C104740

FSC
www.fsc.org

Constable
An imprint of
Little, Brown Book Group
Carmelite House
50 Victoria Embankment
London EC4Y 0DZ

An Hachette UK Company
www.hachette.co.uk

www.littlebrown.co.uk

Dedicated to Steve Dow and his mum, Marie, with thanks for all their sage Cotswold advice – especially on dwile flonking!

Foreword by R. W. Green

I bet you know Agatha Raisin quite well. If you're reading this foreword, rather than skipping it in order to get straight to the story, then I'm pretty sure you're interested enough in Agatha to want to find out a little more. Either that, or you've already read the rest of the book and have come back here to see if there's anything worth reading in this bit. Well, there is if you want to get to know Agatha a little better. There is if you're slightly curious. Agatha would approve of that. Smart people, in her opinion, are always inquisitive, always want to know more.

How do I know that's what Agatha thinks? Well, I count myself as very lucky that I got to know Agatha not only through reading about her investigations, but also by sneakily talking about her behind her back. She would hate that, even if my gossiping partner was M. C. Beaton – Marion – Agatha's creator. When I first lent Marion a helping hand with a book she was struggling, through illness, to complete, she wanted to make sure that I understood who Agatha was and how she got along with all the other characters in and around Carsely.

That's how I came to know, for example, that Agatha has never been a great sports enthusiast – Marion told me. Having lived with Agatha in her head for so many years, she knew everything about her. She was able to describe how, when Agatha was growing up in a Birmingham tower block, she had no time for sport. She was one of the cleverest pupils in her year at school, but she was quite shy, lacking self-confidence and shunning friendship by adopting an abrasive persona to avoid anyone getting close to her. That needn't have ruled out playing hockey or netball, or any other sport that might have taken her fancy. You don't, of course, have to be everyone's best friend to be good at sport, and she definitely has the drive, aggression and will to win. Nothing irks her more than coming off second best, but it was her lifestyle rather than her attitude that ruled out taking any serious interest in sport. She had a number of part-time jobs before leaving school to work in a biscuit factory, saving every penny she could towards the day when she had enough to leave her abusive parents and flee to London.

Just because she had no time for sport, however, doesn't mean that Agatha isn't a team player. In fact, she's quite happy to work as part of a team, as long as the team does things her way. She likes to be in charge because that way she can stay in control of everything that's happening – the best way to avoid having egg on her face and feeling the confidence, which has taken her so many years to build, slipping away.

It might seem strange, then, that Agatha should agree to take part in an archery demonstration, as she does early in *Dead on Target*. Archery, after all, is a major sport. People have been shooting arrows at animals, targets and each other for more than ten thousand years and it's been a mainstream Olympic discipline since 1972. Why would Agatha participate in archery? Because she was put in a position where she couldn't back down, and she was presented with a challenge. Ducking out would mean loss of face and, worse, potential ridicule. Agatha had no choice but to take up the bow. It was her first contact with the Ancombe Archers, but it was not to be her last.

Sport may not be something in which Agatha takes a great deal of interest, but dancing is far closer to her heart. Agatha, Marion assured me, is a very good dancer. She has natural aptitude but also put a great deal of effort into learning how to dance well. At first, I wondered why Agatha would consider dancing important enough to take up her precious time, but Marion was adamant. Agatha learned to dance because she enjoyed it, and she allowed herself to enjoy it because she could justify the apparent frivolity of dancing with an ulterior motive – profit. When she was leading a glamorous life as one of London's top PR consultants, she had to attend lots of posh functions where there would often be dancing. As a proficient dancer, she could make sure she was in control when guiding an inept male client around the floor. She could make him look good – only he would know that she had done so and that, in turn, was good for business.

I did wonder whether Marion had made all that up on the spot just because she'd decided that Agatha was a good dancer, but I wasn't brave enough to challenge her on it. Arguing with Marion would have been like arguing with Agatha – with Marion backing her up. There's no way I stood any chance against both of them.

Agatha's passion for dance did, however, allow me to introduce her to Detective Inspector John Glass, with whom she first danced at Alice and Bill Wong's wedding in *Devil's Delight*. He made a big impression with his proficiency on the dancefloor and waltzed into Agatha's life. Whether he's agile enough to keep up with the quick-stepping Mrs Raisin for very long remains to be seen.

I hope you enjoyed reading these musings on Agatha enough to get this far and that you'll now go on to enjoy her latest adventure – if you haven't done so already!

Rod Green, 2023

An Introduction from M.C. Beaton on the Agatha Raisin Series

The writing road leading to Agatha Raisin is a long one.

When I left school, I became a fiction buyer for John Smith & Son Ltd on St Vincent Street, Glasgow, the oldest bookshop in Britain – alas, now closed. Those were the days when bookselling was a profession and one had to know something about every book in the shop.

I developed an eye for what sort of book a customer might want, and could, for example, spot an arriving request for a leather-bound pocket-sized edition of Omar Khayyam at a hundred paces.

As staff were allowed to borrow books, I was able to feed my addiction for detective and spy stories. As a child, my first love had been Richard Hannay in John Buchan's *The Thirty-Nine Steps*. Then, on my eleventh birthday, I was given a copy of Dorothy L. Sayers's *Lord Peter Views the Body* and read everything by that author I could get. After that came, courtesy of the bookshop,

Ngaio Marsh, Josephine Tey, Gladys Mitchell, Eric Ambler, Agatha Christie and very many more.

Bookselling was a very genteel job. We were not allowed to call each other by our first names. I was given half an hour in the morning to go out for coffee, an hour and a half for lunch, and half an hour in the afternoon for tea.

I was having coffee one morning when I was joined by a customer, Mary Kavanagh, who recognised me. She said she was features editor of the Glasgow edition of the *Daily Mail* and wanted a reporter to cover a production of *Cinderella* at the Rutherglen Rep that evening, because the editor's nephew was acting as one of the Ugly Sisters, but all the reporters refused to go.

'I'll go,' I said eagerly.

She looked at me doubtfully. 'Have you had anything published?'

'Oh, yes,' I said, lying through my teeth. '*Punch, The Listener*, things like that.'

'Well, it's only fifty words,' she said. 'All right.'

And that was the start. I rose up through vaudeville and then became lead theatre critic at the age of nineteen.

After that, I became fashion editor of *Scottish Field* magazine and then moved to the *Scottish Daily Express* as Scotland's new emergent writer and proceeded to submerge. The news editor gave me a tryout to save me from being sacked, and I became a crime reporter.

People often ask if this experience was to help me in the future with writing detective stories. Yes, but not in the way they think. The crime in Glasgow was awful: razor gangs, axemen, reporting stories in filthy gaslit tenements where the stair lavatory had broken, and so, as an escape, I kept making up stories in my head that had nothing to do with reality. Finally, it all became too much for me and I got a transfer to the *Daily Express* on Fleet Street, London.

I enjoyed being a Fleet Street reporter. I would walk down Fleet Street in the evening if I was on the late shift and feel the thud of the printing presses and smell the aroma of hot paper and see St Paul's, floodlit, floating above Ludgate Hill, and felt I had truly arrived.

I became chief woman reporter just as boredom and reality were setting in. That was when I met my husband, Harry Scott Gibbons, former Middle East correspondent for the paper who had just resigned to write a book, *The Conspirators*, about the British withdrawal from Aden.

I resigned as well and we went on our travels, through Greece, Turkey and Cyprus. Harry was now engaged in writing a book about the Cyprus troubles. We arrived back in London, broke, and I had a baby, Charles. We moved to America when Harry found work as an editor at the *Oyster Bay Guardian*, a Long Island newspaper. That was not a very pleasant experience.

But I longed to write fiction. I had read all of Georgette Heyer's Regency romances and thought I would try some of the new ones that were coming out. I complained to my husband, 'They're awful. The history's wrong, the speech is wrong, and the dress is wrong.'

'Well, write one,' he urged.

My mother had been a great fan of the Regency period and I had been brought up on Jane Austen and various history books. She even found out-of-print books from the period, such as Maria Edgeworth's *Moral Tales*. I remember with affection a villain called Lord Raspberry. So I cranked up the film in my head and began to write what was there. The first book was called *Regency Gold*. I had only done about twenty pages, blocked by the thought that surely I couldn't really write a whole book, when my husband took them from me and showed them to a writer friend who recommended an agent. So I went on and wrote the first fifty pages and plot and sent it all to the agent Barbara Lowenstein. She suggested some changes, and after making them I took the lot back to her.

The book sold in three days flat. Then, before it was even finished, I got an offer from another publisher to write Edwardian romances, which I did under the name of Jennie Tremaine because my maiden name, Marion Chesney, was contracted to the first publisher. Other publishers followed, other names: Ann Fairfax, Helen Crampton and Charlotte Ward.

I was finally contracted by St Martin's Press to write six hardback Regency series at a time. But I wanted to write mysteries, and discussed my ambition to do so with my editor at St Martin's Press, Hope Dellon. 'Okay,' she said. 'Who's your detective?'

I had only got as far as the rough idea and hadn't thought of one. 'The village bobby,' I said hurriedly.

'What's his name?'

I quickly racked my brains. 'Hamish Macbeth.'

I had to find not only a name for my detective but a new name for myself. 'Give me a name that isn't Mac something,' suggested Hope. She said that M.C. Beaton would be a good name, keeping the M.C. for Marion Chesney.

So I began to write detective stories. We moved back to London to further our son's education and it was there that the idea for the first Agatha Raisin was germinated, though I did not know it at the time.

My son's housemaster asked me if I could do some home baking for a charity sale. I did not want to let my son down by telling him I couldn't bake. So I went to Waitrose and bought two quiches, carefully removed the shop wrappings, put my own wrappings on with a home-made label, and delivered them. They were a great success.

Shortly afterwards, Hope, who is very fond of the Cotswolds, asked me if I would consider writing a detective story set in that scenic area. I wanted the detective to be a woman. I had enjoyed E. F. Benson's Miss Mapp books and thought it might be interesting to create a detective that the reader might not like but nonetheless would want to win in the end. I was also inspired by the amusing detective stories of Colin Watson in his Flaxborough novels and Simon Brett's detective, Charles Paris.

Agatha Raisin will continue to live in the Cotswolds because the very placid beauty of the place, with its winding lanes and old cottages, serves as a constant to the often abrasive Agatha. I am only sorry that I continue to inflict so much murder and mayhem on this tranquil setting.

Agatha Raisin
DEAD ON TARGET

Chapter One

'I'll kill him! I swear I will! We can't let him get away with this!'

The woman was furious, storming past the refreshments-tent queue with a man in her wake. He reached out to grab her by the arm and she spun to face him, her long blonde hair a swirling mane.

'Just wait!' he pleaded. She was a few years younger than him and for a moment he stood over her, as though he were about to chastise a child, but he quickly relented, attempting to reason with her. 'It's not too late to get him to change his mind. I'll have another word with him . . .'

'Why bother?' she snapped. 'He doesn't listen to you. He doesn't give a damn what we think! The time for talking is past. We have to *do* something! Understand? We have to do something about him!'

'Listen to me . . .' The man looked round, suddenly aware that those waiting in the queue had abandoned their own conversations and the half-finished text messages on their phones to be entertained by the unexpected drama. One woman in particular caught his attention. She had a smooth bob of glossy brown hair and an

1

expression of intense curiosity. He glowered at her. Agatha Raisin stared back at him, her bear-like eyes unflinching.

'Let's talk in the car, my love,' he said as the blonde woman shook her arm free. He urged her towards the nearby car park. 'Too many eavesdroppers around here.'

'Such excitement so early in the morning, Mrs Raisin,' came a voice from behind Agatha, catching her by surprise.

'I was thinking exactly the same thing, Mrs Bloxby,' Agatha replied, turning to greet her friend. It amused them to address each other in public with the customary formality of the Carsely Ladies Society, while in private, over a glass of wine or a schooner of sherry, they were Agatha and Margaret. 'We don't usually see such theatrics at the Carsely Village Fete until well after the beer tent has opened.'

Agatha nodded towards a marquee where staff from the local Red Lion pub were unpacking glasses, stocking shelves with bottles and exchanging friendly banter with a growing huddle of local men waiting patiently in the sunshine, all eagerly anticipating their first pint of the day.

'I hope you didn't take what was being said literally,' said Mrs Bloxby, smiling. 'I'm sure Stephanie isn't about to kill anyone. That's just something people say when they're upset.'

'I know,' Agatha said, 'and something was certainly upsetting both of them. I take it you know them?'

'Yes, Stephanie and Gerald were married here.' Mrs Bloxby looked to the edge of the field in which they were standing, where the steeple of the Church of St Jude poked its spire above the trees. Agatha had never been a particularly religious person, but she had always found the fourteenth-century church, with its stained-glass windows set in mellow Cotswold stone, a gently comforting presence in the village. It helped, of course, that she knew Margaret Bloxby would generally be waiting with a warm welcome in the rectory next door. Her husband, Alf, was the vicar at St Jude's.

'Gerald's father, Sir Godfrey Pride, owns Carseworth Manor, the big house in the woods over there.' Mrs Bloxby pointed to the trees beyond the field in which they were standing. 'His family donated this land to the church for the benefit of the local people. That's why the fete is now held here each year.'

Agatha gazed out over the colourful collection of tents arranged in neat rows around an open arena in the middle of the field. Jolly, candy-striped canvas structures stood shoulder-to-shoulder with sun-bleached white bell tents and traditional ridge tents while tall teepees and elaborate marquees mingled with family campers and basic garden gazebos. Most had trestle tables set up outside displaying a variety of goods from homemade cakes and home-grown fruit and vegetables to children's toys, second-hand tools and flowering plants.

Some tables and tents were overwhelmed with myriad articles that some liked to call bric-a-brac but Agatha called crap. Who really wanted to buy mismatched, discoloured crockery, chipped china ornaments, dull crystal decanters or plastic Buddhas? She could well imagine why people would want to rid their homes of such junk, but how on earth could anyone take delight in buying someone else's junk?

'We seem to have rather a lot of pre-loved treasures for you to browse this year,' said Mrs Bloxby, watching Agatha disdainfully appraising the closest of the bric-a-brac tables.

Agatha gave her friend a sideways glance, aware that she was sporting a mischievous smile. Margaret Bloxby was petite and neat with plain brown hair laced with occasional wispy strands of silver-grey and a kind face well-practised in forming expressions of sympathy and compassion. The impish smile was reserved for teasing Agatha. Although she would never normally tolerate anyone poking fun at her, the slightest spark of provocation easily igniting her infamously short fuse, Agatha could never be angry with Mrs Bloxby. On so many occasions she had provided Agatha with a warm welcome, a patient ear, a shoulder to cry on and sage advice. She had always been a good friend.

Yet what had always impressed Agatha most about Mrs Bloxby was not her gentle, caring nature, which she greatly respected, but her stalwart fortitude, which she hugely admired. She had a heart of gold and a backbone of steel. Was that, Agatha mused, too much metal in one person? No matter – Mrs Bloxby's unflinching courage had saved her more than once. She remembered the time when she had been punched by a man whom Mrs Bloxby had immediately smacked over the head with a jar of homemade chutney. Then there was

4

the gunman who would surely have killed them both had Mrs Bloxby not wrestled the weapon from him and shot him in the chest. He had survived, but Agatha often wondered how Margaret Bloxby would have fared had he not. She had been distraught at the thought of having almost taken another's life. Perhaps sometimes there was an overwhelmingly discordant clash of gold and steel.

'You know how much I hate all that stuff.' Agatha laughed, waving a hand at the bric-a-brac, dismissing the junk along with the disturbing memories. 'Still, I suppose all of this goes towards helping good causes.'

'It does indeed,' Mrs Bloxby agreed. 'One of them this year is the restoration of our old graveyard.'

'I hope you're not going to set all the old gravestones straight. They wouldn't look right in tidy rows. They should stay as they are, all higgledy-piggledy, like a bunch of best pals growing old together, not soldiers on parade.'

'I agree. The restoration work's all about rebuilding the graveyard wall and the paths. Besides, some of the stones are so fragile that they'd fall apart if anyone tried to move them.'

Having reached the front of the queue, Agatha insisted on paying for their coffees and was handing one of the recyclable paper cups to Mrs Bloxby when she heard a jingle like sleigh bells. A middle-aged man walked past wearing a tall black hat, a red neckerchief and a white shirt with white trousers. His hat was decorated with a garland of flowers while red sashes fastened with rosettes

5

criss-crossed his chest. The jingling bells were clustered on straps tied just below his knees.

'Ah, the morris men.' Mrs Bloxby gave the man a cheery 'Good morning!' and a generous smile. 'I've always loved the morris men, haven't you? We should really call them morris dancers now, of course – they're no longer men-only groups.'

Agatha spotted the rest of the dancers in the distance, all similarly attired, approaching from the car park. She squinted at one of the figures. There was something familiar about the way he moved, the way he held his shoulders. It couldn't be, could it?

'Quickly!' she breathed, holding her coffee cup out to Mrs Bloxby. 'Take this!'

In what appeared to be one swift movement, she produced a compact mirror from her handbag, smoothed her hair, checked her lipstick and straightened her dress. She felt a wave of relief that she had chosen that particular dress. The white flower pattern on a black background wasn't too frivolously summery and the skirt reached well below the knee, but the neckline still dropped low enough to provide a certain . . . allure. A white rope belt cinched it neatly at the waist. An instant later, the compact was back in her handbag and she was retrieving her coffee.

'Slick.' Margaret Bloxby nodded her approval. 'What was that in aid of?'

'John!' Agatha called to one of the approaching morris dancers, waving madly.

A tall, well-built man looked towards her and grinned. He removed his hat and pretended to hide behind it as he drew nearer, feigning embarrassment at having been exposed as a morris dancer.

'You never told me you were involved in this!' Agatha chided, wagging her finger in mock rebuke.

'I can explain!' He laughed, stooping to kiss her cheek. 'One of the lads was injured and they asked me to stand in. I might be a bit rusty – I haven't done this for years.'

'Mrs Bloxby,' Agatha said, sweeping a hand towards her in introduction, 'this is my friend John Glass.'

Mrs Bloxby watched Agatha and John exchange a glance and caught a twinkle in Agatha's dark eyes.

'Pleased to meet you, Mr Glass,' she said, shaking John's hand. 'I'm so looking forward to seeing the morris . . .'

She was interrupted by a rapid popping noise followed by a dull boom from the PA system's loudspeakers.

'Good morning, everyone . . .' came a man's voice.

Pop! Boom!

'. . . is this thing working . . .?'

Pop-pop! Boom!

'Well . . . welcome to the Carsely Village . . .'

Pop! Boom! Pop!

'Oh, dear,' sighed Mrs Bloxby. 'Alf's making the announcements. He's quite at home delivering one of his Sunday sermons from the pulpit, but this is well outside his comfort zone.'

The Reverend Bloxby, dressed in a short-sleeved black shirt and black trousers that made him look even smaller and thinner than ever, struggled on, gripping his microphone with knuckles as white as his dog collar. Agatha

7

could see his lips moving as he stood in front of the administration tent, reading from a sheet of paper, but now no sound was coming from the speakers at all. She was surprised at how flustered he seemed. Normally he came across as quite confident and self-assured, almost arrogant. Suddenly his voice came blasting out.

'. . . so we'll have everything from archery and morris dancing to shin kicking and dwile flonking . . . wait . . . what? That can't be right . . .'

The PA system let out a banshee screech.

'Oh, bloody hell!' wailed the reverend.

'I think I'd better go lend a hand,' said Mrs Bloxby, handing Agatha her coffee and hurrying over to her husband.

'Fancy a coffee?' Agatha asked, offering John Mrs Bloxby's cup. 'Margaret didn't touch it and it'll be cold by the time she gets back.'

'Thanks,' John said. 'I wasn't sure if you'd be here today.'

'Nor I you,' Agatha replied. 'I thought you were working.'

'I managed to swap to a late shift in order to help out the lads.'

'Is that a privilege of rank in the police force, Inspector Glass?'

'Not really. You usually need a bit of luck on your side to swing it.'

'I see – so how did you become a morris dancer?'

'Quite by chance, really. Years ago, a couple of friends met a bunch of morris men in the pub and they persuaded

8

us to give it a go. I gave it up when work started taking over.'

'So who was it that was injured? What happened to him?'

'So many questions!' He laughed. 'If I didn't know you were a private detective, I could probably have guessed. My old pal Wayne mistimed a move, slipped and got one of these in the face.'

John held up a stout, smooth stick.

'I take it you don't normally whack each other with batons?'

'Some of the dances involve clashing sticks together. They say ash or hazel make the best sound. It's all part of the fun.'

'Speaking of fun, when are you going to take me out dancing again?'

'I checked with Strangley's. They're having another ballroom night in two weeks. I've already booked.'

Agatha had first met John when they danced together at the wedding of their mutual friends, Alice and Bill Wong, also both police officers. It was the first time in years that she could remember having danced the night away in the arms of a man who neither stood on her toes nor tripped over his own feet. She regarded herself as an accomplished dancer but John, whom she learned had danced competitively when he was a youngster, was impressively elegant and graceful.

Less than a week ago, John had surprised her with dinner at Strangley's, a spa hotel between Mircester and Chipping Camden. Agatha had previously only ever thought of the hotel as the sort of place for hen parties and golfing weekends, neither of which held much interest for her, but John had discovered their special dinner-dance events. The evening had spun on late into the night and she had woken the next morning in her cottage bedroom, lying in John's arms.

'You're an angel,' she said, craning her neck to kiss him on the cheek, and he slipped his arm around her shoulder. 'Steady, tiger,' she added, removing his arm. 'Remember . . .'

'I know . . .' he said, with a resigned sigh, fully aware that Agatha regarded too many displays of public affection as being undignified, slightly vulgar and really only for teenagers, '. . . there's a time and a place for everything.'

'Speaking of which,' Agatha said, 'why do we have morris dancers here today? We're well into autumn and I thought it was something that happened in the spring. Isn't it all to do with fertility rites and suchlike?'

'Not entirely. Cotswold dances traditionally tended to focus on Whitsun, which is at the beginning of summer, but morris dancers have always been out and about on Boxing Day, at New Year – pretty much any time, really. The dances have been performed for centuries. Working men, farm labourers, builders and all sorts got involved because they were paid in cash, food and ale. Nowadays we do it for charity – and the ale!'

'So what was all that about shin kicking and . . . vile thonking?'

'Dwile flonking,' John corrected her and she raised a suspicious eyebrow, half convinced that he was about to try to hoodwink her with some dubious shaggy-dog story.

'They're both real things, honestly.' He grinned. 'Shin kicking's been part of the Cotswold Olimpicks since . . .'

'The Cotswold Olimpicks?' Agatha folded her arms, her head cocked slightly to the right, challenging John to prove that he wasn't simply pulling her leg.

'I kid you not,' John defended himself, smiling. 'The Cotswold Olimpicks are held every year just outside Chipping Camden around the spring bank holiday. The games were first staged in the seventeenth century, long before the modern Olympic Games. There have always been lots of traditional contests – tug-of-war, running races and suchlike – but shin kicking has been part of the games since they began. It's a kind of wrestling. Two competitors face each other, grab each other by the collar and take swipes at each other's shins. You have to try to force your opponent to the ground or get him to surrender.'

'And dwile flonking? Is that also an Olimpick sport?'

'It is nowadays. It involves a group holding hands and dancing round in a circle. The person in the middle of the circle is the flonker and has to dip a stick like this . . .' he held up his morris dancing stave, '. . . into a bucket of ale. The flonker then fishes out a cloth soaked in ale, the dwile, and flings, or flonks, it at the dancers. A dancer who's hit has to drink from the bucket and . . .'

'Don't tell me.' Agatha shook her head with a resigned smile. 'The flonker drinks the ale if no one is hit. It's a drinking game, isn't it? How do you know who's won?'

'No one can ever remember.'

'I take great pride in being able to tell when men are lying to me,' Agatha said, laughing, 'and that's all too ridiculous not to be true.'

'No shin kicking or dwile flonking for me, though,' John said with, Agatha thought, a hint of regret. 'I'm on that late shift tonight and I don't want any injuries before our next ballroom date!' He struck a dance pose, as though holding an invisible partner in his arms, and waltzed off towards the other morris dancers, explaining that he had to 'go through some of the dances with the lads', then he turned, pausing for a second to blow her a kiss.

Agatha watched him join the huddle of white-clad dancers. John seemed very relaxed – far more so than when they had first met. He had always been charming and good company but as they had come to know each other better, she had started to see a man far younger than his fifty-four years begin to emerge. That, she told herself, never one to dim the sparkle of her own personality beneath a cloak of modesty, is entirely down to me – Agatha Raisin. I have made a difference to that man's life. He . . .

'He really rather likes you, doesn't he?' The cultured drawl of Sir Charles Fraith came from over Agatha's left shoulder. She turned to face him.

'I wish people would stop sneaking up on me!' she snapped, suddenly furious at having her thoughts interrupted, especially since Charles seemed somehow to be reading her mind. 'You're the second one today. What happened to a simple "Hello" or "Good morning" to attract someone's attention rather than just blundering up and disturbing them?'

'Sorry, Aggie, I . . .'

'And don't call me that!' Agatha had tolerated the pet name when she and Charles had been close, when they had been lovers, but saw no reason to do so now that they were, at best, uneasy friends.

'Agatha . . .' Charles took a deep breath and a smile etched lines in his perfectly shaved face, the tiniest of wrinkles appearing at the corners of his eyes. There were no such creases on his crisply pressed shirt, his blue sports jacket or his cream trousers. Sir Charles Fraith was, as always, immaculately turned out, with scarcely a lock of his fine, fair hair ever out of place. Even when he was stark naked, Agatha knew from past experience that he was an utterly crumple-free zone. 'Good morning. I apologise for catching you off guard.'

'Feisty little filly, ain't she, Fraith?' said an older man accompanying Charles.

'Feisty little . . .?' Agatha glowered at the man. He was far older than Charles, old enough to be his father, and taller, although most men were, with a voice that had the same upper-class tone. His was tinged with an added croak where decades of cigarettes and whisky had dulled its refinement. 'Who the hell are you?'

'Agatha, this is Sir Godfrey Pride,' Charles explained. 'We are what you might call neighbours.'

'No,' Agatha said firmly, 'you are not what I might call neighbours. It would take a day to walk from where you live at Barfield House to where he lives. Your house is surrounded by over a thousand acres, Charles, so you're never going to have a cup of tea and a chat over the garden fence like what I might call neighbours.'

Neither did they seem the likeliest of chums. Sir Godfrey had a shock of wild grey hair, a ruddy face and bleary eyes peering out from behind dark, shaggy eyebrows. His tweed jacket was scuffed and threadbare at the cuffs and his voluminous, rumpled corduroy trousers had badly worn areas that were faded pink, yet were alarmingly red elsewhere, a bit like the boozy face of the old man himself. He reached out, offering Agatha his hand. She made no move to shake it.

'I am not a filly,' she said coldly. 'I am a business-woman.'

'Meant nothing untoward by it, my dear,' he said, by way of apology, 'and it's your business skills that I'm interested in. I hear you're very good at what you do.'

'The best,' Agatha confirmed, finally accepting his hand-shake. 'I understand that this field is part of your land.'

'It was once,' he said, nodding, 'but everything changes. Only old dinosaurs like me, set in our ways, remain the same. Pride's the name, don't y'know, and pride is the enemy of progress.'

'Sir Godfrey has a problem he'd like to discuss with you,' said Charles.

'Yes, but I won't trouble you with that now,' Sir Godfrey said, smiling softly at Agatha. 'You should enjoy the fete and this lovely weather. The dark days of winter will be upon us soon enough.'

'If there's something I can help you with, then we should arrange to meet,' Agatha said, handing him her business card. 'You can reach me on this number on Monday morning.'

'Thank you, my dear. I shall look forward to talking to you again then. In the meantime, I can see something that needs my urgent attention.' He was looking towards the Red Lion tent, now open for business. 'Care to join me, young Fraith?'

'It's a tad early for me, old chap,' said Charles, 'but I may catch up with you again later.'

Sir Godfrey stuffed his hands in his jacket pockets and bumbled off towards the beer tent.

'What was that all about?' asked Agatha once the old man was out of earshot.

'No idea,' Charles said, shrugging. 'I bumped into him on the way here. Haven't seen the old devil in years, but he asked me to introduce him to you. He needs help with something but doesn't know who to trust. Said he wanted to see if you were the right sort.'

'The right sort?' Agatha felt a wave of exasperation turning to another rising tide of anger. 'Honestly, you people never cease to amaze me. Do you mean the "hunting, shooting and fishing" sort, or the "loyal, obedient servant" sort?'

'His words, not mine,' Charles said, defensively. 'All I think he meant was that he was looking for someone trustworthy.'

'And did I pass the test?' Agatha folded her arms, a look of defiance on her face.

'I should say so!' Charles laughed. 'You stood your ground, demanded respect. You couldn't have been too upset by him, though. You still gave him your card.'

'Business is business,' Agatha said, letting her arms drop and the tension drain from her shoulders. 'How are things going with your new enterprises?'

'Rather well, actually. The new vineyard looks fantastic and the winery is under construction. By this time next year we will be producing our first wine. It's all damned expensive, though. A lot of investment.'

'I thought you'd found business partners to help with that?'

'I've had lots of interest, but most of them want to see things up and running before they commit.'

'Oh, Charles,' Agatha sighed. 'You haven't staked everything on this business, have you?'

Agatha recalled the lean years prior to Charles inheriting a fortune from the family of his deceased wife following their short marriage. He had been what is often referred to as 'land rich but cash poor', after a series of increasingly desperate, utterly disastrous investment schemes.

'Not at all,' Charles assured her, with what Agatha saw as forced nonchalance. 'I've had to spend a bit on essential maintenance around the estate, too, but there's still plenty left in the pot . . . enough to take you out to dinner perhaps?'

'Charles, I . . .' She glanced over to where John was in animated discussion with the other dancers.

'Ah, yes.' Charles nodded. 'Your morris man. I noticed the way you were looking at him.'

16

'I like him a lot. He's a good friend.'

'We were good friends once. Practically inseparable. I miss that . . .'

'A lot of water has flowed under the bridge since then, Charles. There's no going back. That will never happen.'

'Never say never.' He smiled. 'Who knows what the future holds, after all? How is James?'

'I haven't seen or spoken to him in quite a while,' Agatha said. Her last conversation with James Lacey, her ex-husband and next-door neighbour, had been a short, high-volume exchange that had ended with the slamming of their respective front doors. 'I think he must be off on his travels again, writing articles about Bolivia, or Outer Mongolia, or somewhere.'

'Really? I heard that . . .' Charles paused, running a hand through his hair, a sure sign, Agatha knew, that he felt he was on shaky ground.

'You heard what?' she prompted him. 'Come on, Charles, spit it out.'

'No, it's nothing,' he said, quickly. Then, realising that he had his catch on the line, he decided to reel her in. 'Idle gossip, I'd say. Let me find out if there's any truth in it and I can tell you all about it over dinner . . . Monday evening?'

'Dinner,' Agatha said, fully aware that she was being played but peeved that Charles might have heard something about James that she had not. What was it? Another woman? Was he moving out of Carsely? She shook her head, trying to persuade herself that she couldn't care less, but she had to know. 'Dinner only. Call me.'

She marched off, leaving Charles in no doubt that the conversation was over by taking a sudden and avid interest in the nearest bric-a-brac stall.

The events at the fete were soon in full swing and Agatha enjoyed watching the first of the morris dances, which involved energetic hopping and handkerchief waving in time with music provided by an enthusiastic fiddle player and a tiny, white-bearded old man who was almost hidden behind a giant accordion. Despite his misgivings, John never put a foot wrong, as far as Agatha could tell.

There followed an archery demonstration by the Ancombe Archers Club. Six archers – three men and three women – using modern, high-tech bows stood at shooting positions near the middle of the arena, aiming at targets around fifty metres away. There were no spectators anywhere near the targets, and the area behind the targets was a tangle of shrubs and bushes that marked the edge of some woodland. The circular targets had a white outer ring, with a black ring inside it, then a smaller blue ring, a red ring and a gold centre circle. They staged the demonstration as a competition, each archer firing six arrows and the one with the lowest score dropping out until there was just one winner, one of the women. Agatha applauded each stage of the contest along with the rest of the spectators. She was impressed that not one arrow missed the target and amazed at how many of them struck gold. The Ancombe Archers were deadly accurate.

When the archery was finished, Mrs Bloxby could be heard once more on the PA system announcing that anyone interested in archery should join the archers down by the targets for a brief lecture, while the top end of the arena would now host the dog show.

'There will be awards,' she informed everyone, 'for the cutest puppy, the most beautiful female, the most handsome male, and the dog who looks most like its owner. Last year that one was won by Stan the bulldog and his owner, also called Stan. Stan's wife told me that Stan didn't snore as loudly as Stan, but Stan definitely drooled more than Stan – and I never worked out which Stan was the snorer and which was the drooler . . .'

Agatha had never considered herself a 'pet person' until she had been given her two cats, Boswell and Hodge. At first, she had been wary of looking after the animals, but once she realised how independent they could be, which took some of the worry out of having them in the house, and how affectionate they were, which had both surprised and delighted her, she had come to adore them. Dogs, on the other hand, were too much of a burden. She found herself smiling, however, when she saw the gaggle of puppies on leads being walked into the arena. Some trotted along, tails wagging, some bounced around, and some leaped on others, rolling and wrestling in a tangle of leads. Any reprimands from their owners were met with lolling tongues, wide, bright eyes and more tail wagging. They're cute, Agatha admitted to herself, but the archers are really impressive. Those bows could kill – an almost silent murder weapon

– and that makes them far more interesting than a bunch of smelly little puppies!

Agatha strolled over to where a small crowd had gathered around the group of archers. Barriers had been put in place and the spectators were encouraged to stand behind them as two of the archers, one male and one female, set up a target about ten metres from where a bearded man with a cloud of snowy white hair stood holding his bow. Agatha guessed he was in his late seventies, but he stood tall and straight and, once those setting up the target were well clear, he selected an arrow, drew back his bowstring and shot the arrow straight into the centre of the gold circle.

'Good morning, everyone!' the old man said, lowering his bow and turning to the spectators. 'My name's Robin Hood . . .' A ripple of polite laughter flowed from the crowd. 'That always gets a bit of a laugh,' the man continued, grinning, 'but my name really is Robin Hood. You're probably all now thinking, "Poor sod – how could his parents do that to him?" Well, Hood's my father's family name and his first date with my mum was a trip to see the old nineteen thirty-eight Robin Hood movie, so I've always been quite grateful they didn't call me Errol Flynn Hood! In fact, if they'd met a couple of years later, I could have been Pinocchio!'

There was more laughter from the crowd and Agatha smiled. Public speaking was something she'd had to do many times in the past when she had run her own London public relations agency. She had given speeches to gatherings of sophisticated, highly influential businesspeople and had always prepared rigorously beforehand in order to conquer her nervousness. She'd been spurred on by a horrendous recurring dream where she was addressing an audience only to hear her voice slowly revert from the acceptably cultured accent she had worked so hard to perfect to the Birmingham twang that betrayed her roots in a council tower block. Mr Robin Hood, on the other hand, had a natural, relaxed manner that easily charmed his audience.

'So, with a name like Robin Hood, what other sport could I possibly take up than archery?' Robin Hood laughed. 'Now, who would like to give it a go? How about you, young lady?'

It took Agatha an instant to realise that he was looking at her.

'Come along, don't be shy – give her a round of applause, everyone. What's your name, young lady?'

With the eyes of the crowd now upon her and the applause ringing in her ears, Agatha gave Robin her name, taking a tentative step forward to be met by one of the female archers who asked if she was right- or left-handed. On being informed that she was right-handed, she asked for Agatha's left arm and, once Agatha had set her handbag on the ground at her feet, she helped her to strap a leather protector over her inside forearm.

'My Maid Marion will help you with the kit,' said Robin, standing close to the spectators, a few metres to Agatha's right. 'Actually, her name's Petula but none of Robin Hood's rogues were ever called Petula, were they?'

The woman laughed. She was the winner of the archery contest, slender, dark-haired, and Agatha judged her to be in her early forties. She helped Agatha fit a kind of three-fingered glove on her right hand.

'The arm protection stops the bowstring from doing any damage when it's released, Agatha,' Robin explained, addressing the spectators as much as he was Agatha, 'and the finger guards do likewise when you draw back and release. Spider will now show you the bow. He's called Spider because of that spider's web tattoo on his left elbow. For goodness' sake nobody ask him where the spider is – he might show you!'

Spider was a skinny, scruffy individual in his late twenties and only a little taller than Agatha. He showed her how to fit the bow's hand grip in the 'V' between the thumb and forefinger of her left hand.

'The grip allows you to balance the bow there without clutching it too tightly,' Robin explained. 'Then, standing sideways with your shoulders aligned with the target, you can raise your hand to shoulder level, keeping your arm straight.'

Robin demonstrated raising the bow and Spider, standing much closer behind Agatha than she would have liked, gently lifted her wrist until her hand was at shoulder height. As Robin outlined the importance of adopting a 'square stance' with your feet parallel to the target, Spider released Agatha's wrist. His fingers traced a path up her arm, drifting gently down to linger lightly around the side of her left breast. Agatha froze. She could scarcely believe it. Had she really just been secretly groped in front of a crowd of people? She turned her head to glower at him only to see a sly leer on his face.

'Keep your distance and keep your hands to yourself, Spider!' she hissed. 'Or I'll crush you like a bug!'

Undaunted, he remained standing close behind her. Robin was now demonstrating, without actually drawing the bowstring, how the thumb on the right hand should come back to a point just below the jaw.

'You need to keep your body straight,' he said, 'so that your arms are level across your shoulders, forming a "T" shape with your torso . . .'

'Like this?' Agatha asked, bringing her elbow up and flinging it back. She caught Spider just below the nose. He yelped and doubled over, cupping his hands over his face. Some of the spectators winced, others simply burst out laughing.

'Whoops!' Robin called. 'Gently does it, Agatha. You'd best take a step back there, Spider!'

Spider retreated, rummaging in the pocket of his jeans to retrieve a crumpled tissue and stem a faint trickle of blood from his nose.

'Maid Marion, would you take over with Agatha, and give her an arrow, please?' Robin motioned Petula forward.

'He deserved that,' Petula said quietly, lending Agatha a hand to fit the groove or 'nock' at the base of the arrow to the bowstring. 'He's such a creep. Somebody needs to teach him a lesson.'

Agatha looked Petula in the eye, the younger woman returning her gaze from beneath a furrowed brow. With that brief exchange, a moment of dark understanding passed between them. Petula had also suffered from

Spider's unwelcome attention. Petula stepped back, Robin calling out instructions.

'Keep the arrow pointing down the range at the target, Agatha,' he called. 'Now, with your index finger above the nock point, your middle finger and ring finger below, raise the bow. Keep that left arm straight and bend your right arm to draw back the bowstring, thumb below your jaw.'

Agatha did as instructed, looking down her left arm to where the arrow rested on the grip's 'shelf', lining the arrow up with the round target. Then her eyes flicked left, distracted by a yellow shape that had popped into view near the bushes just beyond the target. A young Labrador dog gazed back at her. To her horror, she realised that she was now looking down the arrow, directly at the puppy, and she could feel the bowstring starting to slip on the leather finger guards.

'Oh, please, no!' she breathed, but it was too late. She felt the string release and shut her eyes tight as the arrow took flight.

Chapter Two

Agatha heard a groan from the spectators. She didn't dare open her eyes. For what seemed like an eternity, but was actually only a second or two, she stood with her eyes clamped firmly shut. Then she heard the strangely calm voice of Robin Hood.

'Oh, that's a shame,' he said, 'but it's really not unusual on a first attempt.'

Agatha was confused. What did he mean, 'not unusual'? Surely it wasn't normal for novice archers to murder defenceless puppies? She opened her left eye a crack. The spectators were mumbling among themselves, a few were laughing a little. Nobody seemed at all upset. She opened both eyes. There was no sign of the puppy, but the arrow was embedded in the grass about three metres in front of her.

'Agatha's mistake,' Robin pointed out to the crowd, 'was to push the bow away from her just before she released. The arrow, of course, was then pointing at the ground, and that's where it ended up.'

Agatha could hear Spider sniggering. She turned to face him, firing a poison-tipped glare more deadly than any arrow. The smile disappeared from his face and he held his grubby tissue back up to his nose.

'Why not have another try, Agatha?' said Robin, and Petula handed her another arrow.

'Did you see the puppy?' Agatha asked, keeping her voice low.

'What puppy?' Petula replied.

'So nobody saw ...?' Agatha gritted her teeth. Only she had seen the puppy, so no one knew that she had been distracted. Robin Hood, Petula, Spider and the entire crowd clearly all thought she was a pathetic, useless woman who could do no better with a bow and arrow than to skewer a buttercup. She raised the bow, drew back the string and loosed the arrow. It slammed into the centre of the gold target circle.

There was a loud cheer from the crowd and a clatter of enthusiastic clapping. She felt empowered, vindicated and extremely pleased with herself. She hoped that the smile she beamed at the crowd made her look happy and grateful for their applause rather than simply smug but she didn't much care either way.

'Well done, Agatha!' Robin congratulated her. 'Now, who else would like to have a go?'

Agatha handed the bow to Petula and was stripping off the arm protector when she heard Mrs Bloxby's voice over the PA.

'If I could have your attention, please,' she said, with only the tiniest of metallic screeches from the giant loud-speakers. 'A yellow Labrador puppy called Ossian has run off from the obedience contest. He's very friendly, so if you find him, please bring him along to the administration tent.'

'Would that be the puppy?' asked Petula.

'Sounds like him.' Agatha handed over the arm protector and finger guard along with her business card. 'If you get any more trouble from him,' she said, nodding towards Spider, who was skulking nearby, 'talk to me. I can help.'

Agatha said goodbye to Robin Hood, who told her she was 'a natural' and that if she ever wanted to take up archery, she should get in touch. She assured him she would, and headed for the refreshments tent, intent on rewarding herself with another coffee. Halfway there, however, her stomach let out a thunderous rumble. Checking left and right, she was pretty sure no one had heard, but a secondary gurgling persuaded her the three coffees she had already drunk that morning were probably sufficient and what she really needed was something to eat. The smell of frying onions and warm pastry from the refreshments tent sealed the deal. The onions were being served up in buns with burgers or hot dogs dripping with ketchup and mustard. That, Agatha thought to herself, looks fantastic, but how do I eat it? The last thing I want is a spray of grease or mustard down the front of this dress.

Outside the refreshments tent, a scattering of white plastic tables and chairs were fully occupied by couples who appeared oblivious to the fact that their caterwauling children were running wild at their feet. Inside was equally crowded. Agatha had almost decided to suffer the rumbling rather than submit to the inelegance of attempting to eat with her hands while standing and trying to avoid ruining her dress when she spotted a familiar face behind the food counter.

'Hello, Mrs Raisin!' called Doris Simpson, Agatha's faithful cleaning lady.

'Hello, Doris,' Agatha said. 'What are you doing here? No . . . let me guess . . . your cousin Rita's daughter, Zoe, roped you in to do a bit for charity.'

'Good heavens!' Doris laughed. 'If you wasn't already a detective, I'd recommend you take it up!'

'Well, it wouldn't be the first time Zoe had relied on your help, would it?'

'No, and I'm always happy to lend a hand,' Doris said. 'Now, feeling a bit peckish, are we?'

'I was, Doris,' Agatha sighed, 'but I'm not sure what to have.'

'Then you should try one of these.' Doris passed a hand over a tempting selection of sausage rolls, the flaky puff pastry a crisp golden brown. 'Fresh baked just minutes ago and that pastry light as a butterfly's wing.'

She watched Agatha purse her lips as though testing her lipstick, hesitating at the thought of being seen with disfiguring crumbs of pastry all round her mouth.

'And if you take yourself off round the back of the tent here,' Doris said, lowering her voice and jerking a thumb over her shoulder, 'you can eat it by the bushes in peace and quiet. No one will see you and you can fix your make-up before you come back round.'

'Am I really so obviously shallow and vain?' Agatha said, looking a little hurt.

'Not at all, Mrs Raisin – but if I looked as good as you always do, I'd want to take care of myself, too. No point in short-changing yourself when you look like a million dollars!'

'You're a very good salesperson, Doris!' Agatha smiled. 'I'll have one of those delicious-looking sausage rolls.'

'You won't regret it,' Doris guaranteed, using tongs to slip one of the large sausage rolls into a white paper bag. 'I'll be round to do you on Monday as usual.'

Agatha took Doris's advice and headed round behind the tent where a fallen tree trunk lay near the bushes in a patch of sunlight. Sitting on the log, she unwrapped the sausage roll and took a bite, leaning off to one side to let a flurry of pastry flakes fall clear of her dress. It was every bit as tasty as she had hoped and she devoured it in no time, only pausing with the last morsel in her hand when she heard a rustling from the bushes. Ossian the Labrador appeared by her side, sat down just out of reach and whimpered, looking up at her with the most irresistible hazel eyes she had ever seen.

'I suppose you think I should share this with you?' she said, and he tilted his head a little to one side, his eyes never leaving her. 'You know everyone's looking for you, don't you?' He tilted his head a little more. 'If I give you this, you have to let me take you in. It's what I do, you know. A private detective spends more time tracking down lost pets than tracking down murderers.'

She held out the last piece of sausage roll and he leaned towards her, sniffed at it, gently took it from her fingers and swallowed it in one gulp. She made a move to grab his collar but, swift as she was, he dodged aside as if in slow motion, swaying to avoid her.

'Come on, Ossian,' she said, standing and untying her rope belt, intending to slip it through his collar. 'You have to come with me now. That was the deal.'

Ossian, however, didn't seem interested in Agatha's deal. He padded a couple of paces towards the bushes, watching her follow him. She tutted. No one who knew Agatha Raisin would ever accuse her of losing her patience. Everyone knew she had none to lose.

'Just you come here, you little rat!' she scolded him, but he slipped through a gap in the bushes, whimpering as he went. 'Where are you going – and why are you crying like that? Get back here!'

Agatha brushed aside the foliage, grimaced as she felt some thorny twigs snagging her dress, and followed Ossian onto a path where the bushes, apart from an occasional patch of undergrowth, gave way to trees and a carpet of dead leaves and moss that rolled in green waves over tree stumps and fallen branches. The dog trotted a few metres in front of her, pausing now and then to make sure she was still following.

'What the hell are you playing at, you stupid mutt!' Agatha snapped. 'Can't you see I'm trying to help you? Hold still, will you?'

Ossian waited until she was almost close enough to grab him, then set off again along the path. Agatha cursed, ready to give up the chase and return to the fete where she could report having seen him. Then he'd be someone else's problem. Ossian, however, had other ideas. When he saw her wavering, he barked loudly at her, then sat down, whimpering again.

'What's wrong, boy?' Agatha said, drawing nearer. This time he made no attempt to elude her, but simply whined and whimpered. When she crouched beside him, he let her stroke his head and put the rope through his collar. 'That's better. Now we can get you back to your owners.'

When Agatha stood to lead him away, however, Ossian refused to budge. He dug his paws in and barked again, this time looking off to Agatha's left. Following his eyes through a tangle of undergrowth, she spotted a flash of pink near the base of a wide tree trunk.

'Did you find something in there, boy? Is that what you're barking about? Let's take a look . . .'

Once more, Ossian dug his paws into the leaf litter on the path, holding his ground.

'You don't want to go back in there, do you? All right,' Agatha said, dropping the rope and wagging a warning finger at him, 'I'll take a look, but you stay right here. No more running away, agreed?'

He looked up at her, blinked once and lay down on the path.

'I swear you can understand everything I'm saying,' she muttered, shaking her head in amazement. Then she stepped off the path, picking her way through the tree debris on the forest floor, thankful that the sandals she was wearing had modest, wide heels rather than anything that would sink too deeply into the moss. A low-hanging branch brushed her head and in the few steps it took her to reach the tree trunk, she realised with growing trepidation what the pinkish red colour was. One glimpse of what lay behind the tree confirmed that she was looking at the faded corduroy trousers of Sir Godfrey Pride. The old man lay, still and silent, at the foot of the tree with a trickle of blood coming from the corner of his mouth. An arrow was embedded in his chest. Agatha had seen enough corpses to believe that she was staring at a dead man. She took a step closer. There was a gurgling cough and the old man gasped for breath. He was alive! Agatha was kneeling by his side in an instant.

'Can you hear me, Sir Godfrey?' she said, trying to keep her voice strong and confident. 'Stay still. Don't try to speak. I'm phoning for help.'

Her phone was in her hand and she was poised to dial when he reached out to grip her wrist.

'You . . .' he wheezed, trying to force out breathless words, '. . . fil . . .'

'Yes, Sir Godfrey, I'm the feisty filly. Now I have to phone for . . .'

He gave a weak smile, his hand dropped to his chest and beneath his shaggy brows, his eyes slowly closed.

'Sir Godfrey!' Agatha yelled. 'No! Hold on! I'll get help!'

But it was too late. Sir Godfrey Pride was dead.

Agatha stood and stared at the body. The pink trousers were crumpled round his ankles, his legs bare and pale. There were leaves and moss tangled in his white hair. Agatha recalled his words about 'pride' and sighed. There was no pride in the old man now and, as if to make his passing as demeaning as possible, death had robbed him of all dignity.

'Snakes and bastards!' she said quietly, crouching once again and reaching out to stroke his forehead. 'What the hell happened here, Godfrey?'

She swept aside the wave of sympathy and sorrow that was threatening to force a tear from her eye and tapped a speed-dial number on her phone. Her mind was now full of questions. How could this have happened to the old man? Why would anyone want him dead? What was it he had wanted to talk to her about? Who murdered Sir Godfrey Pride? The phone was answered after four rings.

'John,' she said, 'I'm afraid you'll have to abandon the hopping and jingling. Your late shift is starting early – there's been a murder.'

The arrival of a detective inspector at a crime scene is usually heralded by the blare of a police car siren, but Agatha was far more relieved to hear that John was closing in on her by the tinkle of his knee bells. She waited on the path, holding the rope belt now serving as Ossian's lead. The young Labrador sat at her feet staring intently towards the sound of the bells.

'Agatha!' John said, panting as he ran towards her. 'Are you . . . all right?'

He was more than a little taken aback by her appearance. The dress that had looked so stunning earlier that morning was now devoid of its belt and hanging like a sack from her shoulders. There were muddy patches and

33

knee marks on the front of her dress, a twig dangling at about waist height and a couple of leaves in her hair. What looked like flakes of pastry were clinging to her lipstick.

'Of course I'm all right,' Agatha said, frowning at such a ridiculous question and pointing towards where the body lay. 'It's Sir Godfrey Pride who's got the arrow sticking out of his chest!'

'He's got a what?' John looked to where the body lay, craning his neck to try to see more, then stepped carefully towards the tree. 'Stay where you are, Agatha. I need to check him out.'

Moments later, he was back on the path.

'He's dead all right,' John said, sombrely, 'but his trousers and . . . well, it's all a bit weird really, isn't it? Did you find the body?'

'No, Ossian did.' Agatha nodded at the puppy.

'Ossian?' At the repeated sound of his name, an excited Ossian jumped up on his hind legs, planting two muddy paws on the front of John's white trousers. 'Did you touch anything?' John asked Agatha, calming the dog.

'I'm not exactly a beginner at this sort of thing,' Agatha said, raising a reproachful eyebrow. 'I know exactly how important it is to maintain a crime scene, but I had to try to reassure him while I phoned for help, so I did touch the body.'

'He wasn't dead when you got here?'

'No, but he only had seconds . . .' Agatha's eyes were suddenly wide with alarm. 'Do you think I could have done more? Could I have saved him? CPR or something like that?'

Now the full horror of what she had come across in the woods seemed ready to overwhelm her.

'There was nothing you could do, Agatha.' John put his arm round her shoulder. 'Chest compressions aren't going to work with a wound like that, especially when there's a bloody great arrow in the way. I very much doubt if mouth-to-mouth would have made any difference either by the time you got to him. All we need do now is wait for the uniformed officers and the team from HQ to get here. I'll call it in.'

'What about Ossian?' she said, changing the subject in order to focus her mind on something other than the piteous image of the old man's body. 'His owners must be so worried about him.'

'Phone your friend Mrs Bloxby and let her know that the dog is okay. You'll be able to take him back soon, but in the meantime you both need to stay right here.'

Within a few minutes, uniformed officers had arrived and were securing the scene, tying blue-and-white police tape around trees and bushes. Curious members of the public, alerted by the arrival of the police, began drifting away from the fete towards the woods, crowding against the tape. John instructed the officers to keep them at a distance.

'Glass! What's going on here?' The wheezing, nasal tone announced the arrival of Detective Chief Inspector Wilkes. Tall and skinny, like an undernourished ostrich, he came striding down the path towards Agatha and John. Even above the rustle of the leaves at his feet, Agatha was sure she could hear the crackle of static electricity from the cheap fabric of his brown suit. 'And what on earth are you wearing?'

'I'm off duty, sir,' John explained, 'helping out the morris dancers.'

'Sir Godfrey Pride has been murdered,' Agatha explained. 'His body is lying behind that tree.'

'Agatha Raisin.' Wilkes curled his upper lip, staring at her with mean, beady eyes. 'Always crying "Murder!" aren't you? Always out to grab some attention and get your name in the papers. What are you doing here?'

'Mrs Raisin discovered the body, sir,' John said.

'Actually, Ossian did,' Agatha added.

'Ossian . . . ?' said Wilkes and, hearing his name again, the young dog jumped up, his front paws scrabbling against Wilkes's legs.

'Get that monster away from me!' Wilkes whined. 'Look what he's done to my suit!' He brushed at the paw marks with his hand, as though the suit had come from Savile Row rather than a supermarket sale rack. 'It's this way, is it?' he added, stepping off the path towards the tree.

'Sir, shouldn't we wait for forensics to . . .' John began, but Wilkes simply waved a hand to silence him as he tromped through the undergrowth towards the body.

'I'll decide if we need a forensics team out here,' he bellowed and they listened to him scrabbling around out of sight behind the barrier of bushes. 'Ah, yes . . . I see . . . yes, of course.'

Agatha sighed in despair and was about to yell at Wilkes about contaminating a crime scene when she spotted Alice Wong approaching.

'Hello, Agatha,' Alice said, smiling. She was tall and slim with waves of dark hair framing her face. Even when attending a murder scene, Agatha thought to herself with a pang of jealousy, Alice manages to look absolutely gorgeous.

'Wilkes is blundering around in there,' Agatha said, looking towards the bushes where John was standing, clearly concerned about Wilkes's behaviour.

'Is that DI Glass?' Alice said, slightly thrown by John's unconventional attire. 'I'd best let him bring me up to speed.'

Alice joined John, and Agatha reached into her handbag for her compact. She was horrified by the sight staring back at her from the small mirror. She plucked the leaves out of her hair, wiped her mouth with a tissue and was reapplying her lipstick when John and Alice walked over.

'Why didn't you tell me I looked so hideous, John?' she moaned.

'I'm . . . um . . . just not that brave,' John said, his mind clearly on other things. 'Alice will have to take a statement from you, Agatha, and . . .'

'Just as I thought,' Wilkes announced, emerging from the bushes. 'A tragic accident!'

'What are you talking about?' Agatha moved forward to confront him. 'How could that possibly be an accident?'

'It's my understanding that there was an archery demonstration earlier,' said Wilkes, producing a programme of the day's events from his jacket pocket, 'in the arena, over in that direction.' He pointed the programme further along the path.

'You think one of the archers shot him?'

'Well, it's obvious, isn't it?' Wilkes snorted. 'The old man sneaked off into the woods for a . . . call of nature . . . and he was hit by a stray arrow from the archery demonstration. Then he staggered down here trying to find help.'

'But I watched the archery demonstration,' Agatha pointed out, 'and not a single arrow missed the target.'

'See the whole thing, did you?' Wilkes sneered. 'Watched them warming up before the show, getting their eye in, or whatever these people do?'

'No, I didn't,' Agatha admitted, 'but I'm sure the archers will know if any of their arrows are missing. We need to talk to them.'

' "*We*", Mrs Raisin? I think I need to warn you that this is a police matter now. *You* are not to talk to anyone or interfere in any way.'

'I'll do what I damn well please! This was my client and . . .'

'Your client?' Wilkes's eyebrows shot up his forehead. 'So you're more involved with the deceased and this incident than you have so far led me to believe?'

'I suppose he wasn't *actually* a client,' Agatha started to explain, 'but he said earlier there was something he wanted to talk to me about and . . .'

'Do you know, Mrs Raisin, I think we need to make this conversation more of a formal interview. We should continue our chat at police headquarters.'

'No, no, no.' Agatha shook her head and folded her arms. 'You'll just keep me hanging around for hours and ask me a load of completely stupid questions.'

'If you come in voluntarily,' Wilkes gave her a thin smile, 'it makes things so much easier. Should you refuse, you might give me cause to think it necessary to arrest you . . .'

'Come down to the station, Agatha,' said John, stepping between her and Wilkes in an effort to calm them both down, 'and we can get the whole story straight in no time.'

Agatha sighed and nodded.

'Good,' John smiled. 'I'll come with you and . . .'

'You'll do nothing of the sort, Inspector,' Wilkes butted in. 'It seems to me that you're far too familiar with Mrs Raisin to be involved with any enquiry that may ensue from the unfortunate death of Sir Godfrey Pride. Go home, get changed and report for your shift at the appropriate time, appropriately dressed. You're supposed to be a police officer, not some kind of carnival side show. I don't want you prancing around the station with your little jingly bells.'

John turned to Wilkes, his face etched with fury, but before he could say a word, Agatha put a hand on his forearm, looked in his eyes and gave a little shake of her head. Wilkes was not worth a blemish on his record.

'Yes, sir,' John said through gritted teeth. 'Right away, sir.'

'DC Peters . . . I mean Wong . . .' Wilkes snapped his fingers at Alice, correcting his clumsy use of her maiden name. 'Take Mrs Raisin to HQ in Mircester where she will be helping us with our enquiries. I shall join you once I have finished here.'

Roy Silver sat in an overstuffed armchair in the bay window of his Kensington apartment, trying to decide whether the London weather would tolerate him wearing a light jacket to take a stroll for a late lunch at the Devonshire Arms, or if the forecast showers would catch him out. He had almost decided to take the chance when the phone rang.

'Silver?' The voice was coarse, rumbling with discontent.

'Who's calling, please?' Roy asked quickly, trying to mask the feeling of dread that had hit him like a crowbar as soon as he'd heard the voice. The one word that had been uttered had left him in no doubt who it was.

'Stop messin' me about, Silver! It's Freddy Evans, and you know fine it is!'

'Ah, Mr Evans,' Roy said, hoping he sounded smooth, calm and nothing like the panicked little man in his head who was screaming, *How did he get my home number?*

'You're probably wonderin' how I got your home number,' Evans said, and Roy sank back in his chair, half convinced that the man could read his mind. 'Well, I make it my business to know everythin' about people who work for me, see? I don't like my business bein' messed up by nasty little surprises!'

'Nasty little . . . Mr Evans, I'm afraid I don't know what you're talking about.'

'Well, you should know! I'm payin' you to know! You're the one's supposed to have all the fancy, top-drawer contacts in the Cotswolds! How is it I have to find out about Pride from my own people?'

'Find out about Sir Godfrey? Find out what, exactly?'

'He's dead, you plonker! Murdered, so I hear. Now get your slinky little arse up to Carsely, bend a few ears and find out what the hell's goin' on!'

'Mr Evans, it's not really my job to . . .'

'Your job is whatever I tell you it is, Silver! I got a pile of money ridin' on this deal. You got me into it and if the deal goes tits up, you're the one who'll suffer for it, see? Now get it sorted!'

The line went dead. Roy decided against lunch at the Devonshire Arms, instead pouring himself a generous glass of Chardonnay to help stop his hands from shaking long enough to pack a bag for a trip to the Cotswolds. There was only one person he knew who could get him out of this mess. Freddy Evans might like to think of himself as a hard-nosed businessman, but he was no match for Agatha Raisin!

Alice Wong guided her car carefully out of the lane leading from the field where the Carsely Village Fete was now buzzing with talk of the body in the woods. Ossian had been returned to his relieved owners and on their way to the car Agatha had been approached several times by locals asking if she knew what had happened.

'I can't say anything,' she had repeated over and over again. 'Detective Chief Inspector Wilkes is in charge.'

'This will be the talk of the Red Lion tonight,' Alice said with a sigh. 'Everyone will have something to say about a body being found, until a police officer asks a few questions, at which point they'll all clam up. Nobody will have seen anything. Nobody will know anything.'

'Somebody knows what happened,' Agatha said. 'Poor old Sir Godfrey didn't shoot himself with an arrow. Somebody killed him and it was no accident.'

'Bill always says your instincts often turn out to be right.'

'He's a smart cookie, your Bill. How is he?'

'He's fine.' A little smile came to Alice's face. 'We don't always see as much of each other as we'd like. We work different shifts so that there's never any conflict of interest at work but when our rest days coincide we can sometimes have three whole days together. That's bliss.' She gave a happy shrug.

'I'm glad for you. I take it he won't be working on this case, then?'

'He might. A lot depends on what conclusions Wilkes draws.'

'Wilkes couldn't draw a blob with a crayon.' Agatha let out a hiss of exasperation, thinking of the old man lying by the tree. 'Who would want to kill that poor old man?'

'I don't doubt he had enemies. He may have looked like a harmless old soul, but he certainly had a way of rubbing people up the wrong way. And he had a bad reputation with women.'

'You sound like you knew him.'

'I met him a couple of times. I used to be friends with Stephanie. We went to the same school, although not at the same time. She's a few years older than me. She married Gerald, Sir Godfrey's son.'

'Blonde Stephanie? I saw her with her husband earlier on. She was very upset with someone. The way she spoke to Gerald, I'm inclined to think it was his father. She said she was going to kill him.'

'You know you're going to have to tell all of this to Wilkes?' Alice's shoulders sank a little. 'Don't hold anything back, Agatha. You have to tell him everything.'

'I'll answer whatever questions he puts to me, don't worry. I just wish I knew what it was that Sir Godfrey wanted to talk to me about.'

'Wilkes will want to know everything he said to you.'

'I know,' Agatha said with a frown of concentration. 'If only I could have made out exactly what he said at the end . . .'

'Oh, Agatha.' Alice's voice had a note of despair as she pulled out onto the main Mircester road. 'If Wilkes is forced to treat this as a murder investigation, and you were not only the one who discovered the body but also the last person to see the victim alive . . .'

'Then I will become his prime suspect.' Agatha met Alice's anxious eyes with a look of defiance, leaving the young detective in no doubt that she relished the prospect of crossing swords with the detestable Wilkes. 'He will try to pin the murder on me.'

*　　*　　*

By the time she was walking up her garden path early that evening, Agatha felt exhausted. She had spent hours at the police station, first waiting for Wilkes to return from the woods, then waiting for him to decide he was ready to talk to her, then suffering the interminable interview itself.

'Why did you go to the fete, Mrs Raisin?' he had asked.

'Why does anyone go to a fete?' Agatha had replied. 'It was supposed to be a fun, relaxing day in aid of the church charity. If no one had gone, it wouldn't have been a fun fete, it would have been a failure. You might not know much about fun, Chief Inspector, but you're no stranger to failure.'

'Don't try to intimidate me, Mrs Raisin. Did you go there to meet Sir Godfrey Pride?'

'No. I had no idea he would be there.'

'Yet you did meet him, didn't you?'

'I met my cleaning lady, too, but I'd no idea she would be there either.'

'You've got a smart answer for everything, don't you?'

'Maybe you should try coming up with a smart question.'

The verbal sparring started out as a relief from the monotony of waiting but soon became a tedious endurance test. Agatha ended up answering the questions on autopilot while her mind was elsewhere, planning a chat with Robin Hood; having another talk with Alice; wondering how best to approach Gerald and Stephanie Pride; reminding herself that Charles would be a good source of background information on Sir Godfrey – and

44

what *did* Charles know about James? Still Wilkes droned on, desperately trying to get the upper hand.

'You know, Chief Inspector,' she had said eventually, standing to head for the door, 'I've had enough of this. I've told you everything I know and now I'm simply tired of listening to you trying to show that you're better than me. Hell will freeze over before you could ever manage that. All men who feel the need to prove they're superior to women obviously actually believe that all men are fundamentally inferior. I guess it's a problem you just have to live with.'

Now, having taken a cab home, all she wanted to do was feed her cats, take a shower and have an early night. The cats, as usual, gave an enthusiastic welcome to the provider of food. They wound themselves around her ankles, walking tall with tails high, then both backed away, eyeing her suspiciously.

'What?' She frowned at them. 'You can smell young Ossian, can't you? Are you jealous? You should be – he was cute and clever.'

They forgave her when she walked into the kitchen and reached for their food bowls. Once she'd fed them and fussed over them for a while to make sure they knew that Ossian was not a rival for her affection, she went upstairs to take a shower. She had just slipped into her favourite robe and wrapped her hair in a towel when the doorbell rang. She made her way downstairs and squinted through the front door's new peephole, one of a number of new security devices she'd had fitted after two villains had recently broken in during the night and tried to set the place on fire. She immediately recognised Roy Silver standing on her doorstep. She sighed. Roy wouldn't turn up completely unannounced, without even a phone call, unless he was in some kind of trouble, but she simply couldn't be seen in her present state, not even by an old friend like Roy. She whipped the towel from her hair.

'Wait there, Roy,' she called. 'I'm not decent!'

Towelling her hair, she trotted upstairs to make herself presentable. Less than ten minutes later she was back at the front door, her hair restored to its normal glossy bob and her make-up immaculate. She was wearing a forest-green cotton wrap dress – not one of her favourites but comfortable and quick to put on. She opened the door.

'Surprise!' Roy squawked in a weak attempt at a fanfare.

'It is a surprise, Roy,' Agatha agreed, now able to take a proper look at him. She had known Roy since he had worked for her London PR agency. He had stayed in touch, proving to be a useful contact and a good friend. Yet this was not the Roy Silver of old. He was, as always, dressed in his own inimitable style – a dark blue bomber jacket, blue-and-yellow hooped T-shirt and close-fitting pale yellow chinos that ended just above his ankles, revealing blue-and-yellow spotted socks. His sartorial style might have been vintage Silver, but his face looked as if it had grown old. Despite the tanned skin, he looked pallid, with worry lines creasing his forehead.

'I'm not really dressed for visitors,' she said, pulling the door open wide and motioning him to enter, 'but you look like you need to sit down with a stiff drink.'

'You have no idea how much I was praying to hear you say that,' he gushed, dropping his bag in the hall and hurrying through to the living room.

'Why didn't you call?' Agatha asked, fixing them each a gin-and-tonic. 'It's not like you to arrive unannounced.'

'I've switched off my phone,' Roy said, tossing a smart-phone onto the coffee table. 'I'm sure he's able to listen to my calls.'

'Who is? What's this all about, Roy?'

'I need your help, Agatha. Please say you'll help me. I don't know anyone else I can turn to. If you can't help me, then I'm a dead man!'

Chapter Three

'How does it feel to be the prime suspect in a police murder investigation, Mrs Raisin?'

Agatha had checked the caller's name before answering her phone, so she knew she was dealing with Charlotte Clark, a reporter on the *Mircester Telegraph*. Charlotte had been a useful contact in the past – a valuable source of information – and now she had clearly heard something that had not yet reached Agatha.

'Murder investigation?' she said, with what she hoped sounded like innocent surprise. 'What are you talking about, Charlotte?'

'DCI Wilkes just held a press call and announced that, and I'm quoting him here, "The pathologist's initial findings and certain evidence that has come to light mean we are now treating the body found in the woods near the Carsely Village Fete this morning as a suspicious death."'

'How does that make me the prime suspect?' Agatha asked, determined to find out everything Charlotte knew.

'It's my understanding that you were the one who found the body and that you were the last person to see him alive. Wilkes hasn't released the name of the victim yet, but rumour has it that it's Sir Godfrey Pride and that he was a client of yours.'

'I'm not going to comment on rumours, Charlotte. What is the evidence Wilkes mentioned?'

'He's not saying. Can you confirm that you found the body, Mrs Raisin?'

'Actually, the body was found by a Labrador puppy called Ossian. He led me to the scene.'

'Given that you're already involved, can we assume that you will be launching your own investigation? I believe Wilkes told you to keep your nose out.'

'Wilkes is a fool. I have a vested interest in this case and will be pursuing my own enquiries. I must go now, Charlotte, but let's keep in touch.'

Agatha hung up and sat for a moment, deep in thought. Roy Silver, sitting on the sofa opposite her, remained silent. He knew better than to interrupt her when she was cogitating. He had only just begun explaining how the death of Sir Godfrey had put him in a tricky situation when she had taken the call from Charlotte.

'Finish your drink, Roy,' Agatha said, suddenly leaping to her feet and draining her own glass. 'I need two minutes to change, then we have to get out of here. My guess is the police are already on their way to pick me up again. You can tell me more about your problem once we're safe in the Red Lion.'

As good as her word, Agatha was ready to go in two minutes, having slipped on a pair of black cotton trousers and a black crew-neck cashmere sweater. Her make-up and lipstick were immaculate. Roy marvelled at the transformation.

'I could never get changed that quickly,' he said, 'although you do look a bit like a burglar, sweetie.'

'Good,' she replied. 'It's getting dark outside and I don't want to stand out if we're spotted in the street. You, on the other hand . . . maybe you could change your . . . oh, never mind. Let's go.'

They made their way quickly along Lilac Lane. The lilac trees and bushes after which the lane was named had given up their flowers in early summer and in their place now hung clusters of bulging seed pods. Agatha was fascinated by the changing of the seasons. Even while nature was slipping into the long winter sleep, with all of the death and decay that entailed, the seed pods were evidence of new life, biding its time, waiting for its moment to come in the spring. She always saw them as a symbol of hope – proof that if you kept going and refused to give up, you would win through in the end. She had a foreboding feeling that, before the murder of Sir Godfrey Pride was solved, she would need that sort of hope.

On reaching the high street, they made for the sanctuary of the Red Lion in the gathering gloom, pausing in the shadows near the pub to watch a police car turn into Lilac Lane.

'I suppose I'll have to talk to them again eventually,' Agatha said quietly, 'but not until I'm ready. I need to know more about Sir Godfrey and who might want him dead before I go nose-to-nose with Wilkes again.'

The Red Lion was the kind of English village pub that had oak beams in the ceiling so low they made tall people stoop, and bar stools so high they made short people wish they had longer legs. Agatha had always regarded the stools as redundant pieces of furniture. Perching on one was too awkwardly undignified for her and too precarious for most of the locals after a couple of drinks. She exchanged greetings with a few familiar faces, some of the crowd at the bar even nodding a brief 'hello' to Roy. Strangers in the pub could easily be fooled into thinking that their presence had gone completely unnoticed by the locals, such was the wall of apparently cool indifference they encountered, but the arrival of any visitor was always duly noted, every newcomer surreptitiously assessed by suspicious eyes. More colourful characters could expect to attract more attention, and someone with Roy's kaleidoscope approach to fashion would not normally leave the locals less startled than if he had burst through the pub door riding a pink polar bear. Roy, however, had been in the Red Lion with Agatha so many times in the past, he was now simply seen as one of her more eccentric accessories.

Agatha ordered a bottle of red wine and they retired to a quiet corner to study the menu. The pub's cuisine might never win it any accolades, but its nooks and crannies acted almost like private booths, allowing quieter conversation away from the hubbub of the main bar. They each decided to order steak and chips and Roy began to look a little more relaxed.

'So how are you involved with the death of Sir Godfrey?' Agatha asked, taking a sip of wine.

'You know I go riding over at Tamara Montgomery's stables near Blockley?' Roy answered, accepting Agatha's nod as encouragement to continue. 'I usually manage to get up there a couple of times a month and, of course, we chat a lot.'

'How are the stables doing?' Agatha asked.

'In the black. She's having to take on a couple of permanent staff. Everything's looking good. She was even approached by someone who asked if she might like to set up another branch of her riding school – in Carsely.'

'Let me guess. Might that have been Sir Godfrey?'

'It was indeed. It seems that he was in the financial doldrums and looking for ways to make money.'

'I can understand that. Charles used to be the same. Having a lot of land and a big house doesn't make you rich, especially if your tenant farmers are struggling. How did Tamara's discussions with Sir Godfrey go?'

'They were a non-starter, really. She talked to me about it because I've been helping her promote her business, and she wanted to concentrate on the stables and riding school in Blockley rather than getting involved elsewhere.'

'Did you then contact Sir Godfrey?'

'No, I thought nothing more about it. Then I was approached in a nightclub in London where I often go with friends. One of the bouncers said that the owner wanted to talk to me and there he was, sitting at a table with a bottle of Krug and two crystal champagne glasses – Freddy Evans.'

'Freddy who? I've never heard of him.'

'Mr Evans has a number of business interests – property, leisurewear, racehorses, car dealerships, casinos, nightclubs, security . . .'

'Good grief, Roy, he's a gangster, isn't he?'

'Mr Evans has never been convicted of any . . . yes, I suppose you could call him a gangster.'

'Oh, Roy, what on earth possessed you to get involved with a man like that?'

'He was very persuasive.' Roy gave a heavy sigh and took a sip of wine. 'He offered me a generous fee to help him find the right sort of property where he could develop a spa hotel. I would then also be involved in promoting the new business.'

'So you immediately thought of Sir Godfrey Pride?'

'No, Evans suggested him. He said he wanted the right sort of representative to approach Sir Godfrey. I think he knew that someone like Sir Godfrey would want nothing to do with him, so I was to keep his name out of any discussions. I knew the old man needed money and that rambling old house of his is going to rack and ruin and, as it happened, he was very keen to do a deal. We got into negotiations. Then Sir Godfrey started making noises about backing out.'

'Your Mr Evans wouldn't have been pleased about that.'

'He was livid. He told me to get the deal back on track or he'd make me wish I'd never been born. Then he heard Sir Godfrey had been murdered, phoned me and sent me up here to sort it out.'

They sat in silence as the barman delivered their plates of food, then, once he was out of earshot, Agatha took another sip of wine and smiled at Roy.

'I'd say it's a good thing you're here, Roy.'

'How can any of this possibly be a good thing?'

'Because I can help put you in touch with Sir Godfrey's family, who are the only people who might be able to rescue Freddy Evans's deal. While we're doing that, you will be able to help me investigate the family.'

'You know, normally I'd be skipping with joy at the thought of being involved in a murder case, Aggie, but . . .'

'And,' Agatha continued, carving into her steak, 'you've just provided me with a credible suspect. Who's to say that Freddy Evans didn't have Sir Godfrey bumped off when he scuppered the hotel plan? He might have sent you up here to make it look like he knew nothing about the murder. How did he hear about it, after all? It hadn't been on the news when he phoned you, so who does he have here in the Cotswolds reporting back to him? Eat up, Roy. You're going to need the energy. We've got a lot of work to do over the next few days!'

Gerald Pride slumped into an armchair with a glass of whisky in his hand. He was sitting in the conservatory of his house in Lower Burlip, the most exclusive suburb of Mircester. The house was large and there were many rooms in which he could have chosen to sit, but the conservatory had always been his favourite. It looked out over the extensive garden and made him feel like he was back home at Carseworth Manor. All of the windows in the south side of Carseworth looked out over the green parkland that stretched out towards the woods separating the manor house from the fields of the farms on the estate.

He recalled how, as a boy, he would wake in the summer and dash to his window to see the wide expanse of grass outside sparkling before the sun had chased away the early morning dew. In the winter, freezing mist or heavy frost made him rush to get dressed and run outside so he could hear the grass crunch beneath his boots and watch his breath hang in the air in swirling clouds. When it snowed the whole place looked so fantastically beautiful it left him spellbound. Then he would never walk on the grass. There were other places he could run and play, but the carpet of snow in front of the house had to be kept pristine, with no footprints save for those of an occasional squirrel, rabbit or deer. That way the splendour of it all lasted as long as possible.

Now, however, it was dark outside and he had no view of the garden, just his own reflection staring back at him. He looked older than his years and burdened with the weary sadness of a son who has just lost his father. He watched the reflection of his wife drift into view behind him.

'You're not sitting in here moping all on your own, are you?' she said, cradling a glass of white wine and taking a seat in the armchair opposite her husband's.

'It would appear that I was, my love, until you came along.'

'That's the story of your life, isn't it, Gerald? You did nothing but mope and daydream until I came along.'

'That's a bit harsh,' he snorted, 'even for you. I'm a qualified solicitor, Stephanie – a partner in a law firm. I did a little work off my own bat before you were around.'

'"A little work"?' she quoted him. 'I've never felt comfortable with the way we English understate things as if modesty is some kind of glowing virtue – an excuse to rest on our laurels. With a bit more ambition on your part, we might actually have managed to get out of bloody Mircester by now.'

'This place isn't so bad.'

'This was my parents' house, Gerald. If I hadn't inherited it when they died, I don't know where we'd be!'

'We'd be somewhere else, my love. We wouldn't have done so badly.'

'Well, we can do a lot better now – now that your bastard of a father is gone!'

'Have a care, Stephanie. He was my father, after all, and he didn't deserve to die like that.'

'You weren't exactly on the best of terms, though, were you? I mean, we hardly ever spoke to him without it turning into a blazing row! And if you'd cared that much for him, you wouldn't have done what you did.' She took a swig of wine, stomped towards the door that led into the drawing room, then paused. 'Now that he's gone, I expect you to follow through on the plans we laid!'

He listened to her flounce across the drawing room, her footsteps receding to somewhere else in the house. He didn't care where – as long as she stayed there.

'Not "we", my love,' he said softly to himself, refilling

56

his glass from the decanter on his side table. 'The plans *I* laid – and they may no longer include you.'

Agatha had never considered the Red Lion the area's best place to eat, but it was the closest to her cottage. In the past, she had gladly accepted dishes of steaming hot lasagne or shepherd's pie fresh from the pub's microwave oven, the tastiest morsels being the bits baked onto the dish so firmly that they had to be chipped off with a knife and a great deal of effort. This evening, however, their steaks had been remarkably good and they had just finished eating when Bill Wong walked into the pub.

As a detective sergeant, Bill did not wear a uniform but the locals knew him to be a police officer. A hush descended on the bar when he crossed the room, as though everything they had been talking about up to then involved nefarious criminal activities rather than discussions about the football that afternoon, next year's holiday plans or how apples, chocolate bars and hot cross buns had all been so much bigger and better years ago.

'Hello, Agatha,' Bill said, approaching their table. 'I thought I might find you in here. Hello, Roy.'

Agatha invited him to join them, observing him closely. His mother was a local woman while his father was from Hong Kong, and Bill had grown to become a handsome young man. He had been the first person, apart, perhaps, from Margaret Bloxby, to befriend Agatha when she had moved to Carsely. She had always found him attractive, even when he had a youthful chubbiness, but had always considered him a little too young for her. Now he had a lean, athletic look and, not for the first time, she felt a pang of jealousy towards Alice. Not only was Alice beautiful, tall and slim, able to eat what she liked without ever putting on a single pound – how Agatha wished she had the magic formula for that – but she had Bill as her husband. She was sure she could see a change in him. He looked calm, self-assured and . . . happy. Had marriage given him that in just a few short months?

'Agatha, once again you seem to be at the centre of a whole load of trouble,' Bill said, holding up a hand to refuse a drink.

'I don't go looking for trouble,' Agatha said, defensively.

'Actually, Agatha,' Roy began, 'as a private detective you really do go—'

Agatha glowered at him and he decided to keep that particular opinion to himself.

'I'm sure you know that a car called at your house earlier,' Bill said. 'I guess that's why you're lurking in here.'

'I do NOT lurk!' Agatha was indignant.

'Actually, Agatha,' Roy said, 'as a private detective you often—'

Agatha gave him a look that told him he was on his final warning. He shut up.

'I need you to listen to me,' Bill said, leaning forward a little. 'I'm sorry that you were the one who found the old man this morning. It must have been awful for you, but I know you're strong enough to cope with that. You're also strong enough to cope with Wilkes, which is why I had to come and find you.'

'I knew he'd want to see me again once the penny finally dropped that this wasn't some bizarre accident,' Agatha said, nodding. 'Do you need to take me in now?'

'No,' Bill said, clearly relieved that Agatha appeared to accept the need for a second chat with Wilkes. 'Wilkes will be at his golf club by now, drinking at the bar and telling anyone who'll listen how he's going to wrap up the murder of Sir Godfrey Pride in record time.'

'How does he think he's going to do that?'

'He thinks he's going to pin it on you. He has evidence that he thinks is almost damning enough to charge you.'

'What evidence?'

'I can't tell you that, but he'll probably do so himself if you go to the station to meet with him tomorrow.'

'Tomorrow's Sunday.'

'Wilkes will be in the office from midday.'

'All right,' Agatha said, with a sigh that let Bill know she was far from happy. 'I'll see him tomorrow.'

'Good,' Bill said. 'I'll let him know that you'll be in at one o'clock. Try not to antagonise him, Agatha. I know you didn't kill the old man, but Wilkes will use any excuse to make your life difficult.'

'If he's coming after me,' Agatha said, 'it's him whose life's about to get "difficult".'

As soon as Bill left, Agatha plucked her phone from her handbag and hit the speed-dial number for Sir Charles Fraith. When he picked up, she could hear music, laughter and multiple conversations in the background.

'Charles?' she asked. 'Where are you?'

'A friend of mine is throwing a birthday bash, Aggie,' he replied, his voice booming out of the phone at a volume clearly necessary at the party but too loud for a quiet corner of the Red Lion. 'Are you all right?'

'So far. I need to see you tomorrow morning. Will you be home at Barfield?'

They agreed to meet at ten the following morning. Charles then returned to the party and Agatha turned to Roy.

'I need you to come with me to Barfield, Roy,' she said. 'We have to find out all we can about Sir Godfrey Pride and Charles can help with that. We also need to let him know that Wilkes wants me for the murder. Charles will certainly have been seen with Sir Godfrey this morning and Wilkes will find that out. As far as the bumbling DCI is concerned, that will tie Charles into the murder, too. Wilkes hates him almost as much as he hates me.'

Later that night, Agatha lay awake, listening to Boswell and Hodge gently snoring at the bottom of the bed. She knew she would drift off to sleep eventually, but the turmoil of thoughts buzzing in her head made eventually feel like a long way off. There are so many questions, she told herself, the questions then coming thick and fast. What evidence does Wilkes have? Is it something in the pathologist's report? How could that possibly incriminate me? Is Freddy Evans involved? What was Stephanie Pride so upset about? Who was Morris and did he invent the dancing? Why are Labrador puppies so cute? When

60

visions of puppies scampering around with bells tied to their legs being chased by a giant sausage roll took over, she knew she'd finally fallen asleep.

Barely five miles from where Agatha slept, in a rundown flat above a back-street hardware store in one of the seedier areas of Mircester, the young man known as Spider sat in front of a large TV screen with a game controller in his hands, massacring zombies. At his feet was a half-empty beer bottle. Across the floor were strewn several empty ones, a pizza box, his shoes, a variety of snack wrappers and a selection of video games.

'Spider, when are you comin' to bed?' A weary young woman with short brown hair, wearing an AC/DC T-shirt as a nightdress, appeared in the doorway. 'Aw . . . look what you done. I tidied all your shit up today. Can't you keep it neat? Can't you even try?'

'Try? Yeah, I can try – but how about you try fixin' the mess we're in?' he yelled, dropping his controller and taking a swig from his beer bottle. 'What are we gonna do now the old man's dead?'

'That wasn't part of the plan,' she said, leaning her forehead on her raised right palm, her left hand massaging her lower back. 'How was I to know he'd go and die? Now we need to see what happens next. We need to wait.'

'Wait? That baby ain't gonna wait, is it?' he shouted, pointing at her swollen belly. 'How we gonna get our hands on his money now?'

'I don't know, Spider,' she wailed. 'I can't think now. I'm too tired . . .'

She shuffled back towards the bedroom. He drained his beer, swore and snatched up the controller, blasting another zombie into a thousand pieces.

Sunlight streaming through her half-open bedroom curtains woke Agatha the following morning just before her alarm went off. She rubbed her eyes and threw back the duvet, much to the annoyance of Boswell and Hodge who then had to tunnel out from beneath the folded layer. She was heading for the bathroom when she remembered that Roy was in the spare room across the hall, and reached for her robe in order to avoid any potentially awkward encounter.

Feeling refreshed after a swift shower, she was back in her bedroom trying to decide what to wear before Roy had even stirred. She slipped off her robe and scrutinised herself in her full-length mirror. She congratulated herself on looking pretty good for her age, then looked herself in the eye. 'Liar,' she breathed. Why is it, she asked herself, that age is such a curse? When we're little girls, all we want is to be older so we can have the most fashionable clothes, dine out and party all night. Before we know it, we want to be younger so we can do exactly the same without all this. Her hands each pinched a wodge of flesh just below her waist. 'Steak and chips goes straight to the hips!' she scolded herself.

She tried running on the spot for a minute, then touching her toes until she was overheating so much that she had to stop, unable to spare the time for a second shower. Now she was breathing hard. I blame gravity, she decided. It's had longer to act on those of us who've been around longer, dragging everything down. It starts up here – she slapped herself under the chin a few times to dispel any early morning droopiness in her neck – and then, it gets hold of pretty much everything. I bet gravity hasn't got to Alice and Toni.

'Get a grip, Agatha,' she said out loud to the figure in the mirror. 'They're both young enough to be your daughters, and neither of them will ever have your . . .'

She was silenced by the ringing of her phone and picked it up from the bedside table to see the caller identified as Toni Gilmour. Toni was her most trusted employee, the one Agatha could rely on to keep the business ticking over in her absence, or to back her up even in the tightest of tight spots.

'Good morning, Toni!' she said cheerily. 'I was just thinking about you.'

'Same here,' Toni replied. 'Are you okay, Agatha?'

'What do you mean?'

'Have you seen the Sunday edition of the *Mircester Telegraph*?'

'No, they don't deliver round here since the last paper boy gave up the round. Mind you, he was eighty-two and . . .'

'I'll photograph the cover and send it to you right now,' Toni interrupted. There was a short pause and Agatha's phone pinged. She put Toni on the loudspeaker and downloaded the photograph. The headline read:

with a subheading:

SAYS PRIVATE EYE

and the first paragraph:

> Private detective Agatha Raisin is launching her own inves-
> tigation into the murder of landowner Sir Godfrey Pride
> after branding the senior investigating officer, Detective
> Chief Inspector Wilkes, a fool.

'Oh, crap,' Agatha groaned. 'I've got a meeting with Wilkes at one this afternoon.'

'I think you can count on him not being in a good mood.'

'When is he ever?'

'True. Would you like me there with you?'

'No, I can handle Wilkes, Toni, but if you've got any time today, find out everything you can about Sir Godfrey Pride and his family. He has a son, Gerald, who has a wife, Stephanie. There may be other children, too. I'm going over to see Charles shortly so that he can fill me in on what he knows – they were what they called "neighbours".'

'Okay,' Toni said. 'Good luck. See you in the office tomorrow morning.'

Agatha hurried to dress, choosing a loose-fitting blue trouser suit with a cream silk top. She took care with her make-up, examining the area of her top lip from which she had plucked a couple of sinister dark hairs the day before, making sure none of them was making a come-back. She wanted to look her best for Charles, not because she wanted him back in her life but because she needed him to know that she wasn't letting herself go just because he was no longer around. A girl had to have standards, after all. The suit would also look business-like for her showdown with Wilkes.

'Roy!' she called, rapping on his door before making her way down to the kitchen. 'Rise and shine! I've made the headlines!'

The ornate wrought-iron gates to Barfield House, newly restored and sporting gleaming black paint with gold detailing, stood open, as always. Agatha turned into the driveway where the dark shadows cast by the rhododen-dron bushes as well as the ancient oak and beech trees caused the car's automatic headlights to illuminate.

There was scant relief from the gloom of the driveway when it opened out to reveal the lawns surrounding Barfield House, the morning light dull and flat with the sun hidden behind a low ceiling of heavy grey clouds. Lovers of inspirational architecture would find nothing but disappointment at Barfield. The house itself was a rambling Victorian mansion, designed in a fake medieval style that Charles himself described as 'hardly an archi-tectural gem'. Even the many mullioned windows, which could be relied upon to bring a little life to the building

65

when they caught a twinkle of sunshine, looked sombre and dormant under the overcast sky.

Agatha parked by the steps leading up to the huge, iron-studded oak door and was not surprised to see it open just as she and Roy reached the threshold. Standing in the doorway was Gustav, Charles's loyal manservant, dressed, as was his habit, in a white shirt and black trousers. Gustav liked to think of himself as Charles's butler, but had performed many roles through the lean years, serving as a cook, cleaner, driver, general handyman and gardener. His innate snobbery had always led him to treat Agatha with disdain. As far as he was concerned, she had neither the breeding nor the sophistication to make her a suitable marriage prospect for Sir Charles Fraith and the relationship she had with him was, therefore, most undesirable. The fact that she was no longer involved with Charles gave Gustav no reason to change his attitude towards her, although their mutual devotion to Charles had been the one thing that brought them together as uneasy allies in the past.

'Good morning, Gustav!' Agatha said cheerily, giving him her brightest, most professional smile.

'Oh . . .' was the response she received, Gustav's beady black eyes falling upon Roy. 'You brought *him*.'

'Yes, Mr Silver will be able to make a valuable contribution to my discussion with Charles,' Agatha said, breezing past Gustav into the vast entrance hall, striding towards the library. 'He's in his usual den, is he?'

But when she swung open the tall wooden double doors leading into the library, Charles was not sitting at his desk. She took a few steps into the room, then heard a reedy voice hailing her from a wing-backed armchair by the French windows.

'Mrs Raisin, how kind of you to drop by,' warbled Mrs Tassy, Charles's aged aunt. Waves of white hair framed her pale skin and her forehead wrinkled when she looked up from the newspaper she was reading. 'This isn't my usual Sunday paper, but the headline certainly caught my eye.'

'Yes, you made quite a splash, Aggie,' Charles agreed, walking into the room with a good deal less than the usual spring in his step. His trousers and shirt were neatly pressed and he had not a hair out of place. At first glance, he looked like a man ready to take on the world, but his eyes told a different story. Their pinkish tinge betrayed his late-night carousing. She was about to berate him for using 'Aggie', then decided he looked a little too fragile.

'That's pretty much why I need to talk to you, Charles,' she said, wondering if she had ever seen him look quite so bilious. 'Gustav, I think that some coffee might be a good idea.'

Gustav looked to Charles, who nodded slowly.

'Yes, coffee – a splendid idea,' said Mrs Tassy. 'Then Mrs Raisin can tell us all about the murder of our neighbour.'

The old lady folded her newspaper and eased her tall, slim frame out of the chair, crossing the room to where a sofa and two armchairs were arranged around a coffee table in front of the fireplace. She and Charles took the armchairs, while Agatha and Roy sat on the sofa.

'What the hell happened to the old rogue, Aggie?' asked Charles.

'No, not Aggie,' she replied, pursing her lips and raising an eyebrow in warning. He mumbled an apology and Agatha continued, 'I found him in the woods with an arrow sticking out of his chest. He was still alive then, but there was nothing I could do for him. He died before I could even call an ambulance.'

'An arrow, you say?' Mrs Tassy sounded shocked. She held a hand to her mouth, her eyes showing her distress. 'Poor Godfrey . . .'

'Did you know him well, Mrs Tassy?' Agatha had never seen the old lady look so vulnerable. She was normally rather aloof, always in control, occasionally delivering a sarcastic comment or two and never anything other than defiantly robust.

'I recall him as a young lad,' she said, swallowing hard to bring the slight quaver in her voice under control. 'He was ten years younger than myself – not so much of an age gap when one is in one's twilight years but an absolute chasm in one's teenage years, or early twenties.'

'He would have still been a boy when you were a young woman,' Agatha said.

'Indeed,' the old lady agreed. 'I remember him being so energetic, always running around, laughing, so . . . full of life. It was fascinating to see how he retained all that exuberance and channelled it into everything he did – and he was very dashing as a young officer.'

'He was in the army?' Agatha asked.

68

'Godfrey took the military route, just as his father had done,' Charles explained. 'A commission in the army followed by a job with a City bank to set him straight financially and then early retirement to the country estate to manage his investments.'

Agatha felt Charles was starting to rally a bit now that he was putting some thoughts together and forming a conversation.

'So he didn't always have money worries?' Roy asked.

'Not at all,' Charles said. 'He threw himself into running the estate, but he was also very much involved with the local community. That's when he formed the Ancombe Archers.'

'How on earth did he get into archery?' asked Agatha.

'Godfrey discovered some old book or other when he was exploring the attic over at Carseworth,' Mrs Tassy said, as Gustav appeared, setting cups and saucers on the table and pouring coffee from a tall, elegant china pot.

'Too much time on his hands,' Gustav sniffed. 'Never enough real work to do.'

'That will do, Gustav,' Charles said, waving him away. 'It was a manuscript, in actual fact, handwritten by his grandfather. It purported to be a history of the area. He let me take a look at it once. I took copies of the whole thing.'

'Your Cambridge history degree must have come in handy then,' Agatha commented.

'It certainly helped me to see what the thing really was,' Charles nodded. 'Godfrey's grandfather wrote it some-time in the nineteen twenties. It was utter poppycock – a complete vanity project that put the Pride family at the heart of every historical event in the Cotswolds right back to the Domesday Book in the eleventh century.'

'What does that have to do with the Ancombe Archers?' asked Roy.

'Part of the book . . . manuscript . . .' said Mrs Tassy, 'described how a unit of men known as the Ancombe Archers acted as bodyguards to the king, or queen, when the monarch was in the area.'

'Complete twaddle,' Charles said, taking a sip of coffee and placing the cup back in its saucer with what Agatha noted was a slightly shaky hand.

'Godfrey reformed the Ancombe Archers as a charitable organisation to help disadvantaged children,' Mrs Tassy continued, tutting at Charles. 'He put an incredible amount of time and energy into all sorts of good causes in those days. That's what earned him his knighthood.'

'That doesn't sound like the man I was dealing with,' Roy said, explaining that he had been brokering a deal for the purchase of Carseworth House.

'Godfrey married a very pretty girl, Elizabeth Clifford,' Mrs Tassy said, staring off into the distance as though she could see into the past. 'Related to the Chudleigh Cliffords, so they said. They had two delightful children, but she died twenty-five years ago of some terrible cancer. He loved her very much and he never got over losing her.'

'His son had just started university at that time,' Charles said, 'and his daughter was at Marlborough College. I remember my father talking about how Godfrey was never sober. He let his business affairs slide and things just went from bad to worse. He was left on his own at Carseworth when the staff all drifted away.'

'A sure sign that things are heading for rock bottom,' Gustav said with a sniff, having reappeared as if from nowhere to top up their coffee cups, 'when the servants depart.'

'Like rats from a sinking ship?' Agatha teased him. He narrowed his eyes at her.

'His housekeeper stayed on for a while,' Mrs Tassy explained, 'but there were rumours that she had become more than just a servant. His behaviour even led to a rift between him and his children, especially his youngest. She was called Elizabeth, after her mother.'

'Charles, honey, do I smell coffee?' A young woman with long waves of fiery red hair appeared in the doorway, her eyes closed, sleepily stretching her arms. She was wearing only what was clearly one of Charles's shirts. It was rather too tight to contain her ample bosom and rather too short to cover much else.

'Oooooh . . .' she said, when her eyes opened and she saw everyone staring at her, '. . . people!' She tugged the shirt tails down at the front, causing so much more strain around the chest that one of only two fastened buttons popped off, skittering across the wooden floor. She backed out of the room and her footsteps could be heard scurrying upstairs.

'Oh, Charles . . .' Mrs Tassy made a clucking sound, returning to the window seat and her newspaper.

'Time we were going, I think, Roy!' Agatha stood, slipping her handbag over her arm.

'Aggie ... I mean Agatha ... um ... last night ...'
Charles ran a hand through his hair.

'Yes, the birthday party,' Agatha said, through gritted teeth. 'Was that one of the guests or did everybody get one in a goody bag to take home?'

'No, she's just, well ... about tomorrow evening ...' Charles didn't dare look Agatha in the eye. One glance from her would have left him withering on the spot.

'Let's forget about tomorrow, Charles. After all, you'll have a busy day shopping for a new shirt. Maybe you should shop for a new girlfriend while you're at it!'

Agatha stormed out into the hall with Roy in tow. He paused at the door, turning back to give Charles a sultry smile and a dainty little wave.

'Bye, Charles, honey!'

Chapter Four

'Arrest me for murder?' Agatha gave an incredulous laugh. 'You must be out of your mind, Wilkes!'

'It's Detective Chief Inspector Wilkes, Mrs Raisin,' Wilkes said with a thin smile, resting his elbows on the table. He put his hands together, his fingers forming a kind of church with his forefingers as the steeple. He leaned his chin on the steeple, and his fingers slipped, one of them jabbing his nose. 'You need to show a little respect.'

'Respect, as they say, has to be earned,' Agatha pointed out.

'My rank demands respect from the likes of you!' Wilkes blurted. 'You're lucky DS Wong persuaded me to have this conversation. I'd have done things differently. I'd be quite within my rights to sling you in the cells right now – and don't think I won't!'

'This isn't a formal interview, Mrs Raisin,' said Bill Wong, actually sounding more formal than Agatha had ever heard him before, but using a tone that helped calm his boss. He was the only other person in the spartan interview room at Mircester Police Station. 'You are not under arrest, you have not been cautioned, you are simply helping us with our enquiries.'

'Again,' Agatha added.

'Yes, we appreciate that this is the second time you've come in to talk to us about yesterday's incident and we're grateful to you for that.'

'Certain evidence has come to light, however, that appears to implicate you in the murder of Sir Godfrey Pride.' Wilkes pushed a clear plastic evidence bag across the table. 'Do you recognise this?'

'Of course,' Agatha said, with barely a glance at the bag. 'That's my business card.'

'Can you explain how it came to be in the victim's jacket pocket?' asked Bill.

'Certainly,' Agatha replied. 'I gave my card to Sir Godfrey yesterday morning. He had a matter he wanted to discuss with me, but didn't feel the fete was the right place.'

'So you agreed to meet with him,' Wilkes suggested.

'Not exactly,' Agatha explained. 'I didn't like his attitude at first, but I told him that if there was something he thought I could help with, we should arrange to meet.'

'You admit that you didn't like the man,' Wilkes said, nodding and grinning triumphantly, as though he had laid a trap into which Agatha had stumbled.

'I didn't like the way he first spoke to me, but he didn't seem like a complete pillock,' Agatha said, staring fiercely at Wilkes. 'I know when I'm looking at one of them.'

'You suggested a meeting,' Wilkes said, reaching for a second evidence bag. 'Was this how you arranged that meeting?' He slid the transparent bag towards her. In it was a handwritten note that read:

DARLING G,
MEET ME IN THE WOODS BEHIND THE FETE!
I NEED YOU DESPERATELY!
LOVE,
A
xxxx

'I've never seen that note before in my life,' Agatha assured him, the smile at the corner of her mouth and a little shake of her head showing how astounded she was that Wilkes might believe she had written it. 'If you think I wrote it, then you must also think that I was besotted with old Sir Godfrey. That must surely be the most ludicrous theory you've ever come up with.'

'Not at all, Mrs Raisin,' Wilkes sneered. 'I believe the note was a ruse aimed at luring the victim into the woods where he was subsequently murdered – and the note is signed "A". A for Agatha.'

'Don't be ridiculous!' Agatha could feel a slight flush in her cheeks, her temper starting to rise. 'Lots of women's names begin with "A"!'

'Go on, then,' Wilkes said, clearly relishing the fact that he'd managed to antagonise her, 'name one woman you know whose name begins with "A".'

'My assistant, Toni,' Agatha said.

'Toni begins with a "T",' Wilkes pointed out, smugly.

'It's short for Antonia, you knucklehead!' Agatha snapped, then took a deep breath to calm herself while Wilkes replaced the evidence bags in a beige folder, muttering all the while.

'Is that all you've got?' Agatha demanded. 'What about the pathologist's report?'

'I am not prepared to reveal the contents of a confidential report to the likes of you,' he said, standing to leave the room. 'That will be all for now, Mrs Raisin, but don't think I'm finished with you yet!'

'He must be crazy to think he could arrest me on such flimsy evidence,' Agatha said to Bill once Wilkes had left the room.

'He was ready to give it a go, though,' Bill replied with a shrug. 'He said he wanted to rattle your cage and see what fell out.'

'He really is a fool.' Agatha laughed. 'How did you persuade him not to go through with the arrest?'

'I told him the truth,' Bill said. 'I told him that there was no way we would be able to stop you from conducting your own investigation and, in doing so, you would either get into so much trouble that he would have genuine grounds to arrest you, or you would worry the murderer into making a move that would give him away. Either way, Wilkes gets the credit for wrapping up the case.'

'There's no way I'll ever give any credit to that clown!'

'Think about it, Agatha, and play the smart game. I have to deal with DCI Wilkes on a daily basis now, and sometimes letting him think that he's winning is the best way to get things done.'

76

'You're a smart cookie, Bill,' Agatha said, beaming a genuine smile of admiration. 'Alice is lucky to have you.'

'I'm the lucky one,' he said with that same twinkle of happiness in his eyes Agatha had seen in the Red Lion the previous evening. Bill Wong seemed serenely contented.

Agatha drove home wondering if Roy had managed to accomplish either of the tasks she had set him when they had returned to her cottage after the farce at Barfield House. She turned off the A44 towards Carsely, the road dropping down into an avenue of trees whose branches reached out from the roadside, forming a high tunnel. Swirls of fallen leaves formed golden vortices as she drove by until she reached the first of the village's yellow stone walls.

Turning into Lilac Lane, she could immediately see that Roy had done as he was asked. Toni's car was parked outside her cottage, meaning that he had been able to contact her and that she was joining them for lunch. Agatha hoped that indicated Roy had also managed to book somewhere – his second assignment – because the lasagne TV dinner she had in the freezer wouldn't stretch to three. Getting a table last-minute was a tall order and she hoped Roy had managed to do better than the Red Lion. She'd eaten there so often recently she could practically recite the entire menu . . . backwards.

'No time to waste, sweetie!' called Roy, scampering down her garden path just as she closed her car door.

Toni was right behind him. 'It's the Horse and Groom at Bourton-on-the-Hill. We need a quick turnaround.'

'I don't mind driving,' Toni called, jingling her car keys.

'Thank you, Toni,' Agatha said with some relief. 'It's been a weird day. I'll tell you all about it when we get there.'

They squeezed into Toni's little car and were soon zinging back up through the tunnel of trees to the A44. Heading towards Moreton-in-Marsh, they quickly passed a sign for Sezincote.

'Ever been there?' asked Roy from the back seat. 'I went to a wedding there once. It's magnificent, like an Indian palace transported to the Cotswolds, complete with an onion-dome roof and elephant statues in the garden.'

'Really?' Agatha sounded surprised that such an exotic venue could be almost right on her doorstep. 'Must pay it a visit. Slow down on this downhill stretch, Toni. The pub's not far.'

The canopy of trees, only slightly wider than the one over the road leading down into Carsely, suddenly opened out, presenting a view down towards Moreton and the first of Bourton's stone buildings, one of which was the Horse and Groom. Toni spotted what looked like the only available space in the car park and they made their way round to the main entrance at the front of the building.

Outside, the pub had the look of a typical Cotswolds coaching inn, with stone walls and white-painted window frames beneath a tiled roof. Inside was a busy gastro pub and, taking a quick look at the large rear garden, Agatha was surprised to see some hardy souls sitting at tables, enjoying views stretching down to distant swathes of green fields and woodland. She was glad they would be sitting inside, where there was a comforting log fire, black-painted ceiling beams a good deal higher than the Red Lion, stripped stone walls mixed with areas of pleasing pastel-painted plaster and furniture in a sensible, traditional style that made you want to sit down and eat.

Neither was she disappointed with the menu. She ordered Severn and Wye smoked salmon with horseradish cream, followed by a hearty Sunday lunch of pork loin with crackling, Yorkshire pudding, roast potatoes and all the trimmings. Tomorrow, she thought, would be a better day to start her next diet regime.

'Toni, we need to bring you up to speed on the murder of Sir Godfrey Pride,' Agatha said as Roy poured them generous measures of Beaujolais Villages. Toni sipped a glass of sparkling water. 'Roy, tell her all about your Mr Evans.'

Agatha enjoyed her wine while listening to Roy, then turned to Toni.

'I need you to know everything that we do, Toni, so that when we start hunting down the murderer, none of us misses anything important. When we go into the office tomorrow, we'll get Patrick and Simon to carry forward our normal cases while we concentrate on this investigation.

'So, here's what's been happening to me over the past two days . . .'

Agatha started with her arrival at the fete and her first meeting with Sir Godfrey. She had reached the point when she was taking part in the archery demonstration before Toni interrupted her.

'Spider,' Toni said, 'with the spider's web tattoo – I know him.'

'Were you also a victim of his wandering hands?' Agatha asked.

'No, we grew up on the same council estate. He was brought up by his mum, until she died. No one ever knew his father, but she used to work at Carseworth Manor, before it went downhill. I heard that his girlfriend now works there part-time.'

'What was he like, this Spider?' Roy asked.

'He wasn't that different to a lot of the other boys. He got into a bit of trouble – graffiti, shoplifting, drunkenness, that sort of thing. I think they hoped that getting involved with the Ancombe Archers group would do him good, but he's never made anything of himself as far as I know.'

'The archers were set up to help disadvantaged kids,' Agatha said. 'He'd have been a prime candidate, especially if his mother worked for Sir Godfrey.' Agatha paused while their food was served, enjoyed a mouthful of salmon, then carried on. 'So when I was ready to shoot, this little puppy appeared and I had no choice but to fire the arrow into the ground to avoid hitting it,' she said, embellishing the story slightly without feeling that she was actually telling a lie, 'but when I had another go . . .'

*   *   *

In a small, terraced house in Comfrey Magna, a young couple sat in their kitchen, eating macaroni cheese and contemplating the scattering of unpaid bills on the table in front of them. She was slim, with a pretty face, green eyes and long brown hair. His hair was also brown, almost shoulder length, and his eyes were blurred behind glasses with thick lenses and dark frames.

'We have to talk to Gerald, Benny,' she said, her soft, refined accent betraying an expensive education. 'We need money now. We can't wait until all the mess is sorted out.'

'Ain't much I can do about that, Liz,' the young man answered, his slow drawl telling of a less privileged upbringing. 'I'm fine for talking to him, mind, but he's your brother and he don't have much regard for me.'

'He's not inclined to talk to me, either,' she said, 'but he really has no choice. I'm not afraid of him or his stuck-up cow of a wife. All I want is what's rightfully mine and, until I get it, he's simply going to have to bail us out.'

'What if he don't want to?'

'I shall give him no choice in the matter. Either he helps me, or I intend to make life very difficult for him.'

'We needs to tread careful, Liz. Lots of people are all riled up about how your old man died. Lots of people will be lookin' for someone to point the finger at.'

'You're right . . . but Gerald will certainly be on any policeman's list of suspects, and he won't want to attract any undue attention to himself, so now may be the very best time to put pressure on him.'

'If you say so, Liz. I'll back you up whatever you decide, you know that.'

'Yes, I do know that.' She reached across the table to take his hand. 'You are the one thing, the one person, I've always known I can rely on. Tomorrow, then. We'll track him down tomorrow.'

Early the following morning, having parked her car in its usual spot, Agatha was walking along Mircester High Street, admiring herself in each shop window she passed. Mircester did not have many stores in which she chose to shop, and only one reasonably upmarket department store where she had occasionally bought clothes, most of which found their way to a charity shop, unworn, when her mood turned against them. Instead, when she felt the need for some serious retail therapy, she would catch a train to London to visit her favourite boutiques, or even venture a little further and stroll along the Rue Saint-Honoré in Paris. There she would set herself a strict budget that she would subsequently delight in demolishing completely.

This morning, however, she was rather pleased with the fuchsia double-breasted coat dress she had recently acquired in the Mircester department store. The sales assistant had assured her that it was 'mega-chic' and 'almost the very exact same as what that Kate Middleton wears'. Well, if it was good enough for Catherine, Princess of Wales, then it was probably worth the consideration of Agatha, Private Detective.

The neckline dropped low enough for her to wear a cherished gold necklace and for it to be comfortable enough to wear indoors, while the hemline on the knee made it warm enough for the changeable autumn weather outdoors. She had paired the outfit with shoes that boasted a heel high enough to give her the lift and shape she wanted in her calves, thighs and bottom, helping to defy the effects of the dreaded gravity.

She gave the shop window reflections her seal of approval, striding out with confidence towards the old lane where the Raisin Investigations office sat above Mr Tinkler's antiques shop. When she reached the corner, however, her heels clattered to a halt on the pavement. There was a 'thing' tied to a lamppost outside the antiques shop – an animal, big-and-hairy, black-and-white.

She tiptoed across the lane's cobbled road surface to take a closer look, albeit from what she considered a safe distance.

'Mrs Raisin! Is this something to do with you?' Mr Tinkler's round, slightly stooped figure appeared in his shop doorway.

'No, I've no idea what . . .' She took a cautious step towards the creature then stopped when its eyes widened, its ears flattened and it made a grumbling noise. It then gave a little screech and spat a wodge of green slime at her. To her horror, the foul-smelling gunk splattered the front of her dress and she was disgusted to feel little blobs of it hitting her neck. She stepped back, scarcely able to believe what had just happened.

'It did that to me, too,' said Mr Tinkler, opening his jacket to reveal a green-stained shirt. 'This shirt's ruined.'

Agatha turned away, unable to speak, making faint gasping sounds and holding her hands out from her sides as if she couldn't bear to touch herself. She made her way upstairs to the office, where Patrick Mulligan and Simon Black were standing by Simon's desk, drinking coffee.

'Morning, boss! Tell us all about the murder on . . .' Simon's cheery grin faded to a look of confusion. 'Wow! What happened to you?'

'Good grief!' Patrick, a retired police officer, was not easily shocked, but the sight of Agatha shuffling, zombie-like, into the office covered in goo caught him completely off guard.

'There's . . . there's a thing,' Agatha breathed. 'A thing downstairs.'

'What sort of a thing?' Patrick asked.

'It's . . . sort of like a cross between a sheep and a horse,' was the best Agatha could manage.

'A sheep and . . .' Simon leaped to his feet and rushed over to the window. 'Yes!' he crowed, punching the air with delight. 'It's Rocco! That must be the shortest case ever!'

Agatha watched him grab his phone and rush downstairs.

'What the hell is he talking about?' She looked to Patrick and he raised two hands in a calming gesture, recognising the notorious Raisin temper beginning to boil through her shock.

'Maybe you'd like to get cleaned up,' he suggested, taking a step towards her. 'Let me help you with that coat.'

'It's a coat dress, Patrick,' she growled, backing away from him, 'and I'm not wandering around the office in my underwear!'

'Ah, yes . . . I see . . .' he said, then rummaged in a bag beside his desk, pulling out two plastic bags. 'These should fit. Not really you, of course, but . . . emergency wear . . . temporary. We can explain about the "thing" when you're ready.'

Agatha took the bags and headed for the office's small bathroom. She emerged ten minutes later devoid of gunge, her make-up restored, and wearing a blue-and-yellow Mircester United hoodie with matching tracksuit bottoms. She had a bag containing her ruined coat dress in one hand and her high heels and handbag in the other. Toni arrived in the office just as Agatha was about to confront Patrick and Simon. She stared at Agatha, transfixed.

'Umm . . . trendy,' was all she could think to say.

'Temporary,' Agatha growled, disappearing into her private office. She opened the bottom right-hand drawer of her desk, producing a pair of sports shoes she kept for power walking when she was on one of her periodic fitness fads. These, she decided, would work far better with her new leisurewear than her high heels. She made a quick phone call to the department store, establishing that they still had a coat dress in stock identical to the one covered in monstrous animal vomit and festering in a plastic bag by her desk. She paid by credit card and assured them that someone would come to pick it up within the hour, then walked through to the outer office, taking the plastic bag with her. She dropped it in Simon's lap as he sat at his desk.

'Get rid of that,' she said and handed him a note bearing the name of the salesperson she had spoken to about her new dress. 'Put it in a bin outside on your way to pick up my new dress.'

'Why me?' Simon wailed. 'I mean, it's the ladies' department and . . .'

'Because you are responsible for me having to buy a new dress,' Agatha explained, perching on the corner of Toni's desk. 'Now you can explain to me what that monster was downstairs.' She paused, narrowing her eyes in a stern look of warning. 'And this had better be good!'

Agatha's secretary, Helen Freedman, hurried into the main office, hung up her coat, apologised for her bus from Evesham running late, did a brief double take at Agatha's Mircester United supporters' kit, and promised to fetch her a coffee immediately.

'Well, it all goes back to Friday afternoon,' Simon began. 'I was last to leave the office and a phone call came in from a Mr Potts. He breeds llamas on his farm and Rocco, his prize stud – that's a male llama – had gone missing.'

'I see,' Agatha said, accepting a cup of coffee from Helen, 'and how did Rocco know to turn himself in to us?'

'Rocco was brought here by whoever kidnapped him,' Patrick explained. 'Simon did a little ringing around on Saturday.'

'I got a list of names from Mr Potts and did a bit of research myself,' Simon said, 'then I phoned everyone I could find who had anything to do with llamas or alpacas – they're a bit like llamas only smaller – or any other kind

86

of unusual livestock. I told them that Agatha Raisin was on the trail of Rocco. Of course, most of them had heard of you because of the case with Wizz-Wazz the donkey, and the case with those smiley kangaroo things, and most of them said, "Well, God help whoever's got Rocco!"'

Toni laughed. Agatha remained stony-faced. Toni covered her smile with her hand.

'So who *did* have Rocco?' she asked.

'That I don't know,' Simon said. 'It's likely that whoever took him is a breeder who wanted Rocco to give his females a . . . I mean to breed with his herd. It's not easy to sell a llama like Rocco, after all, without everyone in the llama world getting to know about it. I reckon old Rocco has had a fine time over the weekend and, because Mr Potts happened to be in town this morning, he's collected him and they're now on their way back home.'

'What if whoever kidnapped him had decided that, once Rocco had fulfilled his purpose, he was of no further use? A liability, in fact,' Agatha said. 'They might have simply bumped him off once they thought we were after them.'

'They could have done that anyway,' Patrick said. 'Simon reckoned that word would get around the llama-owning community pretty quickly and that, being animal lovers, the kidnappers would want to return Rocco rather than harm him or risk being caught in possession.'

'Friday night to Monday morning!' Simon whooped, doing a little hand-clapping, finger-snapping move and pumping both fists in the air. 'Fastest case clear-up ever!'

Agatha stared at him, impassive, unsmiling.

'Ah, except that . . . of course, it wasn't actually a case,' Simon said, looking sadly deflated. 'I know we all have to clear new cases with you but I couldn't get hold of you and I . . . well, Mr Potts is over the moon and wants to know how much he owes us.'

'We will certainly be charging him for a new dress,' Agatha said, coldly.

'Mm . . .' Simon said. 'Llamas can do that if they feel threatened.'

'And a new shirt for Mr Tinkler,' Agatha added, turning to Patrick. 'What is this I'm wearing?'

'It's hookey merchandise from Mircester United Football Club,' Patrick replied. 'You'll remember that last week we discussed helping them track down the people who've been selling this fake gear and counterfeit stuff from other clubs around the stadium. Most of the fakes are being sold in street markets and the like, but pinning down market traders to make them spill the beans on who supplies them is like wrestling with eels.'

'The clubs are losing a fortune because of this racket,' Simon added, 'but finding who is getting the fakes into the stadium could be the easiest way to track down the source.'

'I see,' Agatha said, plucking at the sleeve of her hoodie. 'Not very good quality, is it? I certainly can't sit around in this all day. All right, Simon, off you go, and as soon as you get back, we'll have a catch-up meeting. Roy Silver will be joining us for that.'

Simon picked up the plastic bag and headed for the door.

'And, Simon,' she said, almost as an afterthought, 'I'm not too happy about the way you used Raisin

Investigations to intimidate people. We are private detectives, not hoodlums.'

The young man's thin face suddenly seemed even longer and he stared at the floor, unsure what to say, then decided that saying nothing was his best option.

'On the other hand,' Agatha went on, 'you got Rocco back, and in this case I think the end justifies the means, so well done for that. Good job.'

He looked up and grinned. How easy it was, Agatha mused as she walked back into her office, to make someone happy. Just a few words chosen with care could make someone's day. Equally, a few carelessly chosen words could ruin someone's life. Sometimes they could do both. She remembered when James had paid her an impromptu visit at a time when she had been feeling utterly depressed. He had been about to leave, then had said, quite casually, 'I actually came round to ask you to marry me.' Those few words had immediately made Agatha the happiest woman in the whole of the Cotswolds, the whole of Britain, the whole world. Yet, as things transpired, those words had also ultimately been responsible for making them both thoroughly miserable when their marriage hit the rocks.

Where *was* James? She tutted at herself for letting his absence irritate her. Even though they weren't exactly on speaking terms, he could have had the decency to let her know he was going away, and for how long.

She returned to her office, busying herself with some paperwork until she heard a tap at her door and Roy Silver popped his head round.

'I've just arrived, sweetie,' he said brightly, then his voice dropped an octave or two. 'Oh, my . . . what *is* that you're wearing?'

'It's temporary!' Agatha snapped. 'Get yourself a coffee and grab a seat outside, Roy. We'll be starting the meeting shortly.'

She stared at the papers on her desk – bills, invoices and reports – without really seeing any of them. Now that the shock of meeting Rocco was wearing off, her mind was back on the murder of Sir Godfrey Pride. Most murders, she told herself, were committed by someone known to the victim. Female victims were more likely than males to be killed by a partner or ex-partner but males were still commonly killed by someone they knew. They had to get to Sir Godfrey's family. No doubt Wilkes would already be on to them.

Then there was the murder weapon – an arrow. Did that have some significance? Her team would be able to help her find all the answers, and they'd certainly get to the truth before the despicable Wilkes. She decided to call the meeting to order in the main office. The addition of Roy would make it all a bit too crowded around her own desk.

'All right, everyone,' Agatha said, returning to her perch on Toni's desk. 'Current caseload. Let's start with you, Patrick.'

They worked their way through the handful of ongoing divorce and surveillance cases on the books. Patrick outlined the plans he and Simon had come up with to infiltrate the group of vendors operating in and around

Mircester United's stadium by posing as the new guys taking over a burger and hot-dog business in the ground. With the backing of the club's chairman, they would then try to spot how the counterfeit merchandise was getting into the ground on match days and who was selling it. Roy listened patiently, clearly enjoying hearing all the artifice and intrigue.

'Apart from Simon and that Rocco creature, anything else new this week?' Agatha asked.

'A sweet old lady called Mrs Parsons rang,' Toni said. 'She has her diamond wedding anniversary coming up with a big family celebration planned and she's thinking of cancelling the whole thing because her husband is acting strangely.'

'What does she think he's up to?' Agatha asked.

'He disappears in his car for a couple of hours once a fortnight on a Tuesday afternoon. Apparently, he comes home smelling of perfume.'

'So she suspects he's having an affair. How old is he?'

'They're both seventy-nine.'

'You'd think he'd know better after sixty years of marriage,' Patrick said.

'Some men never learn,' Agatha responded. 'Let's see if we can straighten this out before the big celebration. Patrick, you and Simon have enough on your plate with the Mircester United case. Toni and I will deal with Mr Parsons. Now – let's move on to the murder of Sir Godfrey Pride.'

Before she could begin to bring Patrick up to date with everything that had happened, there was a knock at the office door. She looked up to see Sir Charles Fraith standing in the doorway.

'Good morning, Ag . . .' he began, then paused and frowned. 'What on earth are you wearing?'

'It's temporary!' Agatha snarled. 'A bit like your Little Miss Buttonpopper, no doubt. Managed to shake off the hangover by now, have you? What do you want? We're actually rather busy at the moment. If it's dinner you're after, you can—'

'This is important,' he said, his stern look and sombre voice taking Agatha a little by surprise. She had thought he might have come to apologise for the previous day but clearly saying sorry was not what was on his mind.

'You'd better come into my office, then,' she said, leading the way and closing the door behind them. 'So who was the redhead? Just another notch on your bedpost or another marriage prospect – the frontrunner in the Lady Fraith Stakes?'

'Shut up and listen, will you?' Charles barked. Agatha pursed her lips, staring at him. He looked angry, or rather, concerned. She folded her arms, sitting back in her chair to hear him out. 'I thought you should know,' he continued, 'that I spoke to a friend of mine – a surgeon at Mircester General Hospital. She told me that James is in the hospital, one of her patients.'

'James?' Agatha was taken aback. 'But how . . . why?'

'You remember when he disappeared off to France after being diagnosed with a brain tumour?'

'Yes, yes, of course . . . but the tumour went away.'

'Well, now it's back with a vengeance.'

'I need to see him,' Agatha said, getting to her feet and picking up her handbag.

'One coat dress as ordered, boss!' Simon breezed into the room carrying a neatly wrapped paper parcel.

'Thank you, Simon.' Agatha brushed past him, taking the parcel and heading for the bathroom.

'Aggie, let me come with you to the hospital,' Charles said. 'If there's a problem with you getting in to visit him, I might be able to, you know, pull a few strings.'

'Thank you, Charles,' Agatha said, softly. 'That would be very kind.'

Half an hour later, Agatha's heels were clicking on the polished floor of one of Mircester General's many corridors. Places like this, she reasoned, were where they made sick people better, so why did the bright lights, the shiny surfaces and the very particular, unmistakeable hospital smell fill her with an overwhelming feeling of foreboding? The smell actually made her feel ill. Even if you needed to be there, she decided – in fact, especially if you needed to be there – a hospital was not a nice place to be.

They approached the reception desk, where a young woman with a pleasant smile looked up from her computer screen and asked if she could help.

'I'm here to see my husband,' Agatha said. 'James Lacey.'

The young woman's fingers tapped at her keyboard before she looked up with a slight furrow in her brow.

'According to the details I have,' she explained, 'Mr Lacey is unmarried.'

'Mrs Raisin is Mr Lacey's ex-wife,' Charles said. 'I spoke to Mrs Shelley this morning and she said Mrs Raisin was welcome to visit.'

'In that case,' said the young woman, her smile returning at the mention of the surgeon's name, 'he's in a room off ward ten. If you speak to the nurse on duty, she'll show you in.'

When they reached James's room, Agatha asked Charles to wait outside. The nurse went in ahead of her and Agatha heard a brief exchange before she returned.

'He's very tired,' the nurse explained, 'but he's happy to see you. Please don't stay too long. He needs to rest.'

The room was more dimly lit than the rest of the hospital and Agatha approached the bed slowly, unsure quite what to expect. The figure of James, normally tall and robust, lying in the hospital bed seemed like a much smaller man, as though he had somehow shrunk. His face, usually sun-bronzed from his many trips abroad as a travel writer, was almost as pale as the hospital bedsheets.

'Agatha, my dear.' He smiled at her and made to raise his head from the pillow.

'Don't try to move, James,' she said, hurrying to the bedside. 'The nurse says you've got to rest.'

'It's good of you to come,' he said.

'Why didn't you tell me you were going into hospital?' she asked, holding his hand. 'I had no idea.'

'I didn't want to worry you with my problems.' He gave a small sigh. 'I'm sorry. I suppose I should have said

94

something rather than just disappearing – and I should have known you would find out what was going on. You're very good at finding things out.'

He smiled and squeezed her hand.

'To be honest, it was Charles who heard you were in here. He said . . . he said the tumour . . .'

'Ah, yes, the old enemy – I mean the tumour, not Charles – back to do battle again. I'm afraid they say it's not going to disappear this time like it seemed to before.'

'You mean when you ran off and I tracked you down to that monastery in the South of France? You've always wanted to deal with your problems on your own, haven't you? You should have let me help you, James. You know I would have.'

'I believe you would, but there's really not much you can do, my dear. They can't operate on this thing in my head, so I'm not going to be here for much longer.'

'Oh, James!' She swallowed hard, trying to stem a growing tremor in her voice. 'How long . . .'

'Three days at the most.'

'Three . . .? But that's terrible!' She buried her face in the sheets by his hand and burst into floods of tears.

'Terrible?' he said, sounding puzzled. 'Wait a minute, Agatha. Did you think . . .? Calm down and listen to me. They can't operate but they've been giving me drugs that are shrinking the tumour. That's been making me feel exhausted, but once they've stabilised the medication, I'll be able to go home.'

'So you're not going to . . .?'

'Die? Well, of course I am. Everyone dies eventually, but I've no intention of doing so any time soon. I'll have to stick with the medication forever but it will help me fight this thing, keep it small. I'll be going strong for years to come.'

'Thank heavens! James, if there's anything I can do to help, anything at all, just say the word.' She dabbed her eyes with a tissue, saying a silent 'thank you' to Helene Winterstein, remembering once reading that she had invented waterproof mascara. Then she shook her head, scolding herself for thinking of that. Why did such irrelevant things pop into your head at all the wrong times? She smiled at James. 'I know we don't always see eye-to-eye but I couldn't bear the thought of you not being around any more.'

'And I couldn't bear the thought of never seeing you again. I guess that's what makes us the best ex-husband, ex-wife team ever to live next door to each other!' They both laughed and she stayed chatting with him for a while longer until the nurse came in and insisted that James be left to rest.

During the short car journey back to her office, Agatha explained James's condition to Charles, who drove in silence, listening intently. He looked over to her from time to time, marvelling at the transformation. The Agatha he had driven to the hospital had been despondently quiet. Now she was talking like an over-excited teenager, full of hope and sparkle, so happy that James would survive. She could be argumentative, self-centred, stubborn and terrifyingly foul-tempered, but underneath it all, Agatha Raisin wasn't entirely the tough nut she liked everyone to think she was.

He wondered if, after all they'd been through, she would still feel as strongly about him as she clearly did about James, should he ever find himself in James's situation. Would she rally round to support him, or would she just give up on him? When she stepped out of his car, thanked him for finding out about James and flashed him a huge smile, he knew the answer. Of course she would be there for him. Agatha Raisin never gave up on anything or anyone!

Chapter Five

Agatha paused in the office doorway, watching Toni and Roy attaching photographs to a large pin-board on the wall. Patrick and Simon were out on the Mircester United case. She studied Toni and Roy working together for a few seconds. The two knew each other well and had worked together before, but were still an odd mix. They couldn't have been more different.

Toni was young and pretty with smooth, pale skin, blue eyes and long blonde hair. She had the effortless beauty of youth that Agatha envied so much it made her stomach ache, especially when she stood anywhere near Toni and felt obliged to squeeze hard on those tummy muscles. She may be slim, Agatha thought to herself, probably even a bit on the skinny side, but she lacks the sort of curves that give a real woman her sex appeal.

Roy was a good deal older than Toni but it was their clothes that made the most immediately apparent difference between the two. Toni lacked confidence, at times seemingly unaware of her own beauty, making her taste in clothes quite unimaginative, while Roy never dressed with anything other than unbridled flamboyance.

'Charlotte at the *Telegraph* was able to help with a few photos,' Toni explained. 'This was Sir Godfrey's wife, Elizabeth, who died when their children were still teenagers.'

'She's very striking,' Agatha noted. 'A beautiful woman.'

'Here's Sir Godfrey in the middle, of course,' said Roy, 'and this is his son, Gerald, along with his wife, Stephanie.'

'I saw them at the fete. What about Sir Godfrey's daughter?' Agatha asked.

'We don't have a photograph of her yet,' Toni said.

'This is Freddy Evans,' Roy said, pinning up a picture of a grim-faced man with eyes narrower than a shrew's snout. He quickly backed away from the photo, but found those eyes following him wherever he stood.

'And this is an old shot of Carseworth Manor.' Toni attached an image of a two-storey building that looked around the same age as Barfield House but was smaller and far more attractive, with fewer windows. Unlike Barfield, where the slate roofs smothered the building like a damp shroud, the slopes of Carseworth's roofs created pleasing angles and every aspect of the house was in sympathetic proportion.

'We should pay Carseworth a visit, Roy,' Agatha said. 'The house is at the heart of your problem, after all.'

'Indeed,' Roy agreed. 'Shame that such a beautiful place should be causing so much trouble.'

'We don't actually know that Sir Godfrey's death was anything to do with the house,' Toni pointed out.

'That's true,' Agatha said, nodding, 'but his property may be the only thing worth killing him for. Money is a powerful motive for murder, but at the moment we don't know what the actual motive for his murder was, although we do have a couple of suspects.'

Agatha tapped the photograph of Stephanie Pride.

'I clearly heard Stephanie say "I'll kill him", and I'm pretty sure she was talking about Sir Godfrey. Whether she meant it literally or not, that still puts her in the frame. Evans may have a motive in that, if Sir Godfrey quashed his spa hotel deal, he lost a lot of money,' she said.

'But he didn't lose any money. He hadn't invested anything in developing the leisure business yet,' Toni reasoned.

'He won't see it that way,' Roy said. 'He will have worked out how much he stood to make, and if he can't then make that profit, he'll count it as money lost – and he'll blame me.'

'Then there's this.' Agatha wrote out the text of the note Wilkes had shown her, drew a big question mark beside it and pinned the paper to the board. 'Who wrote this note? Who is "A" and were they having an affair?'

'When you found him, Sir Godfrey had his trousers round his ankles,' Roy said. 'Was he perhaps caught with his lover by a husband or boyfriend?'

'Could be,' Agatha said. 'Jealousy and revenge are also both powerful motives.'

'But why would he agree to meet someone in the woods at the village fete with lots of people around when he lives alone in that huge house?' Toni asked.

'Maybe it was for the thrill of it,' Roy suggested, 'or maybe whoever he was meeting couldn't get to the house without arousing suspicion.'

'I doubt it,' Agatha said, shaking her head. 'Like everything else to do with Sir Godfrey's death, there's something very wrong about the note. It feels like a complete fake to me. It's all written in capital letters – a good way of disguising your own handwriting. I think the note was to lure Sir Godfrey into a trap.'

'Why the arrow?' Toni pondered. 'It's a strange way to kill someone, isn't it?'

'Good question,' Agatha agreed, drawing an arrow on a piece of paper and sticking it on the board. 'Wilkes may be right in thinking that the murderer intended to make it look like an accident – like Sir Godfrey was shot by a stray arrow – but I'm fairly sure the forensic evidence he wouldn't show me scuppers that theory. So why an arrow and where did it come from?'

'There are a lot of unanswered questions,' Roy said.

'No, not unanswered questions, Roy,' Agatha said, wagging a finger at him to make her point, 'leads to follow. Here's the plan. Toni, I want you to start finding out more about Carseworth Manor. We know there was a plan for a spa hotel and leisure facility and, if there was one plan, there are likely to be others. Official planning applications are public documents but unofficial enquiries – somebody simply testing the water with the planning authority – are sometimes just verbal phone fishing. Are you still seeing young Edward? He works at the local council, doesn't he?'

'We're still friends.' Toni nodded, cautiously. She was always slightly defensive when it felt like Agatha was probing into her love life.

Agatha took in her mood in the blink of an eye. Toni's reticence surely meant that she and Edward were still involved. She hated it when Toni was in a relationship. The job they did often meant working long hours and she liked having Toni at her beck and call. Boyfriends just got in the way.

'Good,' she said quickly. 'Ask him if he knows anyone in the planning department who might be able to shed some light on Carseworth. Also, dig up as much background as you can on Sir Godfrey's financial situation and his children.'

'Gerald is the one I'm most interested in,' said Roy. 'He's the eldest, he's a lawyer, and he's the one who'll take over the spa deal.'

'You and I shall talk to Gerald,' Agatha agreed. 'We'll also visit Robin Hood to find out more about the arrow.'

'I'll try to track down some of the people who used to work for Sir Godfrey as well,' Toni said. 'A former employee with a grudge might have a motive for murder.'

'Good thinking, Toni,' Agatha said. 'Right, let's get out to Carseworth, Roy.'

Agatha drove out of Mircester with Roy in the passenger seat. The day was warm but overcast, occasional gaps in the clouds allowing the sun to brighten the landscape, turning recently harvested bales in the fields into rolls of pale gold.

'It always seems like we're hurtling towards the end of the year,' Agatha commented, 'when those giant rolls of straw start appearing in the fields.'

'That's hay, not straw,' Roy corrected her.

'What's the difference?'

'Straw is a by-product from a cereal harvest,' Roy explained, 'the stalks of wheat or barley, or whatever. It has practically no nutritional value, so it's used for animal bedding – like on the floor of a horse's stall. Hay is a rich mixture of grasses, maybe with a little alfalfa in there – good food for horses and cattle.'

'You've learned a lot from your trips to the stables, haven't you?'

'I find it all quite fascinating, sweetie. I'm a dedicated urbanite, as you know – a confirmed city dweller – but learning to ride with Tamara has made me appreciate the countryside. I love it out here in the sticks, and I absolutely adore horse riding. I was riding a fabulous grey mare last time who—'

Roy fell suddenly silent. At first Agatha was relieved, thankful that she didn't have to listen to another of his excruciatingly detailed horse yarns. Then she looked over at him and saw the look of dread on his face.

'What's up?' she asked. 'You look like you've seen a ghost.'

'If only,' he whispered. 'Did you see the car on the other side of the road?'

'The black Jaguar,' Agatha said, squinting in the rear-view mirror to see the car disappearing in the direction of Mircester. 'What of it?'

'That was Freddy Evans's car!'

'Nonsense, Roy,' Agatha said. 'This is the Cotswolds. There are a lot of wealthy people living around here. Black Jags aren't so unusual.'

'If you say so,' he said, without much conviction.

'I need you to keep your eyes peeled once we're round this corner,' Agatha told him, trying to get his mind back on the job. 'There's a camera in the glove compartment. We should try to get a few shots of the house and its surroundings.'

Roy flipped open the glove compartment and a split bag of dry-roasted peanuts showered its contents onto his lime-green chinos. He tutted, retrieved the long-lensed camera and slammed the glove compartment shut, then vigorously brushed peanut dust off his trouser legs, managing only to create obstinate stains.

'Can I claim dry cleaning on company expenses?' he grumbled.

'Only in extreme circumstances,' Agatha said, bluntly.

An old wooden sign pointing up an overgrown lane confirmed their arrival at Carseworth Manor. Unlike the driveway that swept through the avenue of trees on the approach to Barfield House, the muddy, pot-holed lane was barely passable, with thorny vegetation spilling onto the track from either side. Agatha spotted a gap on the right, narrowing to a path that led off into the woods. The gap was just big enough for her to park.

'Let's walk from here, Roy,' she said. 'I don't want to get the car stuck in this lane.'

'You're going to walk – in those?' Roy eyed her high heels.

'No,' she said, stepping out of the car. 'I have welling-ton boots in the back.' She looked across to see him examining his own footwear – tan brogues with white 'Gatsby' inserts. 'Oooh . . .' she said, cooing in mock sympathy. 'You're going to walk – in those?'

Two minutes later they were trudging towards the house, she clumping through muddy ruts in her floral-patterned rubber boots and he picking his way with great delicacy, the camera slung over his shoulder. Closer to the house, the track swung right and Agatha held up a hand, military style, warning Roy to halt.

'Shh,' she hissed as he opened his mouth to speak. Pointing through some low-hanging tree branches, she made a camera-clicking motion with her hand. Roy peered through the foliage and saw two men and two women standing in front of the impressive oak doors. He levelled the camera at them and brought their faces into focus. Gerald Pride was standing with Stephanie at his side, but the other couple was standing at the wrong angle for their faces to be clear. What was certainly clear was that an almighty row was raging.

The row ended when the unknown woman slapped Gerald in the face and turned away from him. Roy then caught a good shot of her face. Gerald went to grab her but the woman's partner stepped in. He was taller and bulkier than Gerald. A shunt in the chest with the butt of his hand sent Gerald stumbling backwards to land in a heap on the front steps of the house. The couple then jumped into a battered old Land Rover and sped off down the driveway. Agatha and Roy stepped off the track, watching the car buck and roll through the muddy ruts, hitting a soft spot just as it passed them. Agatha was horrified to see the nearest front wheel of the Land Rover plunge into a deep rut, sending a spray of clinging mud and black leaf mulch flying into the air. Before she had time to react, she heard a noise like a brief, soggy round of applause and felt what seemed like a hundred mud balls splatter her new pink coat dress. She winced when she felt a final dollop of cold mud splat on her left cheek.

'Twice . . .' she breathed, stunned into statue-like petrification. 'Twice in one day . . .'

'This doesn't happen in Kensington,' Roy whined, scooping a dollop of mud out of his eye.

'Did you get it?' Agatha asked.

'Oh, I got it all right!' He spat mud off his lips.

'I meant a photo of that fight.'

'So did I. I've got snaps of the whole thing,' said Roy. He sighed, surveying the splatter marks on his pastel outfit. 'Are these cleaning circumstances extreme enough for you?'

'Without a doubt,' Agatha said, wiping the mud off her face with a tissue. 'Now let's go find out what it was all about.'

They strode up to the front of the house, where Gerald was picking himself up off the steps and Stephanie was berating him for being such a wimp.

'Who the devil are you?' he said as they approached. 'And what are you doing with that camera?'

'We're . . . twitchers,' Agatha said, desperate for some sort of cover story that might help them catch the Prides with their guard down. She hoped she sounded more confident than she felt. 'You know . . . bird watchers. We stopped our car because we thought we saw a lesser spotted . . . um . . .'

'Peanut warbler.' Roy stepped in to help. 'In that tree up there.' He aimed his camera at a tree back in the lane and snapped a photo.

'Lesser spotted peanut warbler?' Gerald scoffed. 'Never heard of it.'

'They're very rare,' Agatha explained, 'because they like to eat peanuts and . . .'

'Then they warble . . . and choke,' Roy said.

'We don't have peanut bushes in the Cotswolds,' Gerald frowned, 'and anyway peanuts grow underground and . . .'

'Yet more reasons why these lovely little birds are so rare around here,' Agatha said. 'We stopped to try to take a photo but somebody came flying past in a Land Rover, covering us in muck, so we wondered if you might let us clean up a bit.'

'Cut the crap!' said Stephanie. 'I know you. I've seen your picture in the paper. You're that Agatha Raisin!'

'Guilty as charged,' Agatha said, turning on her most professional smile, 'but we'd still really appreciate the chance to clean up.'

'Now I remember you. You're the one from the fete, the one who found my father, aren't you?' Gerald said, eyeing Agatha suspiciously. 'You'd best come inside. If Elizabeth did that to you, the least we can do is offer you a cup of tea.'

'Elizabeth,' Agatha mouthed silently to Roy as they followed the Prides up the stairs. She scanned the front of the house on the way in. There was moss on the roof and evidence of the gutters leaking. Paint was flaking from the window frames and weeds were sprouting here and there from the pointing around the stonework. Inside, the once-elegant décor was also showing signs of wear and tear. There was oak panelling in the hall to waist level, but the wood looked dull, having lost its lustre. The extravagantly patterned wallpaper above it was torn and peeling in places, and the rugs on the floor looked like they pre-dated the invention of the vacuum cleaner yet had never seen one.

Despite all of that, and the faintly musty smell, the house had an undeniable grandeur. The place reminded Agatha of Charles's aunt – dignified but slightly decrepit, bags of class but a bit crumbly.

Agatha followed the others up the hallway, past a carved oak staircase, to the kitchen at the back of the house. Stephanie provided damp cloths for Agatha and Roy to sponge off the worst of the mud while Gerald made tea. By the time they all sat at the wooden kitchen table, the mud was reduced to stains rather than clods.

'So what were you doing in the lane? And don't give me any more of that claptrap about peanut birds,' Gerald said.

'Actually, we wanted to take a look at the house,' Agatha said. 'We didn't expect anyone would be here. Roy is a long-time associate of mine and had been involved in negotiations with your father to buy the place.'

'What kind of negotiations?' asked Gerald.

'I was engaged by a London businessman,' Roy explained, 'to help him acquire the house.'

'The hotel deal,' Stephanie said, nodding smugly at her husband. 'The deal the old fool should have leaped at.'

'Have a care, my love,' Gerald said, calmly and clearly. 'My father was murdered only two days ago. Show a little respect for the dead.'

'My client's offer is still on the table,' Roy pointed out. 'There's still a deal to be done.'

'I think not,' Gerald said, sipping his tea. 'My father had a change of heart.'

'What made him change his mind?' asked Roy.

'He did!' Stephanie pointed an accusing finger at her husband. 'He started filling the old man's head with nonsense until he didn't know whether he was coming or going! He eventually lost it completely and said we could all fight it out over the house once he was dead and gone!'

'Sadly, that came about a lot sooner than he expected,' Agatha said. 'I take it you had an alternative proposal, Mr Pride?'

'That's not something I'm prepared to go into at this time,' Gerald said.

'At this time? It's too damned late now, isn't it?' Stephanie pushed back her chair, its legs squealing on the tiled kitchen floor. 'You're pathetic. All you had to do was get him to sign the will. Now the whole mess is going to drag on for years!'

She thundered out of the room.

'You must excuse my wife,' Gerald said. 'This has been a traumatic period for all of us.'

'I'm sure it has,' Agatha said in a sympathetic tone, although Gerald didn't seem in need of sympathy. He had a calm, almost chilling demeanour but he wasn't acting like he was going through a 'traumatic period'. In fact, he didn't seem at all disturbed by the death of his father or the shocking manner in which he had met his end. 'You must be terribly upset by what happened.'

'Of course,' Gerald said. 'Losing my father in such a dreadful way has been very difficult.'

'May I suggest to my client that we might resume our discussions once you've had time to come to terms with your loss?' Roy said, hopefully.

'You may not,' Gerald said. 'The idea that this house might be turned into some kind of vulgar beauty parlour makes my flesh creep. This is my home. It was once a fine house, and it will be so again.'

'You've got to be kidding.' Stephanie appeared in the doorway, a glass of white wine in her hand. 'How are you going to run a house like this? You can't cope with a place this size without staff, and who would want to work here? Everyone knows the way your darling daddy treated the servants. Sorry, did I say "servants"? Wenches might be a better term, because there were no men, were there? Just women – and that pervy old goat couldn't keep his hands off any of them!'

'I think you had best go now,' Gerald said, standing.

'Should you ever have need of my services,' Agatha said, placing her card on the table, glancing towards Stephanie and then lowering her voice. 'We're very good on divorce.'

Gerald showed them to the door, then called softly to Agatha as she walked down the steps.

'Mrs Raisin, you were with him when he died,' he said. For the first time Agatha detected what she thought was a note of grief in his voice. 'Did he . . . suffer? Did he say anything?'

'He was beyond suffering when I found him,' Agatha said. 'All that he said was, well . . . earlier that day he had called me a "feisty filly" and that's what he was trying to . . .'

'Yes, that certainly sounds like him,' Gerald said, shaking his head. 'Goodbye, Mrs Raisin.'

Toni was on the phone when Agatha and Roy walked back into the office. Her eyes widened when she saw the mud smears that covered them both. Agatha simply barked, 'Don't ask!' and marched over to a wall mirror.

'The Princess of bloody Wales never has to go through this,' she muttered, scrubbing at the dried-in stains with her fingers.

A few minutes later, both she and Roy were sitting in the outer office, each wearing matching counterfeit Mircester United hoodies and sweatpants. Roy had a sheaf of photos in his hand, printed from the digital camera. Toni stood at the pin-board.

'Sir Godfrey Pride,' she said, tapping his image, 'was flat broke. I found someone who once worked at Carseworth but left when he was no longer able to pay her wages.'

'Did she work there recently?' Agatha asked.

'A few years ago,' Toni replied. 'He hasn't had anyone working there for months. I tracked her down through people I still know from my old housing estate. She said that Sir Godfrey once had a maid, a housekeeper, a cook and a gardener – all women. His wife used to refer to them as "his little harem".'

'According to Stephanie,' said Agatha, 'that's precisely how he treated them.'

'There was a fairly high turnover of staff,' Toni said, 'especially after his wife died. Most left after being groped or having had to fend off other unwelcome advances from the old man.'

'Did no one report him to the police?' Roy asked.

'While he still had money, it appears he paid the women not to make a fuss,' Toni replied, 'but at least one had charges brought against him a few years back, and he was given a suspended sentence. Charlotte sent me a cutting.'

Toni pinned a short newspaper court report to the board beside Sir Godfrey's photo.

'He really wasn't a very nice man, was he?' Roy said.

'No, he wasn't,' Agatha agreed, 'but he wasn't unique, either. There was a time when men thought behaving like he did was just a bit of fun. Some still do. They've really no idea of the humiliation and distress they cause.'

'Some do,' Toni shrugged, 'but they do it anyway. They're the worst. Like Spider, who you ran into at the fete, Agatha. It turns out that his girlfriend cooked and cleaned for Sir Godfrey, just like his mum did. She was the last person to work at Carseworth.'

'Could the murderer be one of the women who worked for Sir Godfrey?' Roy suggested. 'A resentful former employee taking her revenge?'

'That's possible,' Agatha agreed, 'although this doesn't feel like someone from the past. The note that was found on him makes me think the murderer is from the present, not the past. I keep seeing him lying there with the arrow sticking out of his chest and there's something not right about that picture in my head.'

'He had his trousers down,' Toni pointed out.

'Yes, that was all really weird,' Agatha said, 'but there's something I can't quite put my finger on . . .'

'Let's take a look at these,' Roy said, stepping forward to pin some pictures on the board. 'Carseworth Manor – you can see how rundown it's become. Elizabeth Pride – smacked her big brother across the face during a huge argument. I think this must be her boyfriend.'

'That will be Benny. Benny Lambert,' said Toni. 'They live over in Comfrey Magna. He works as a labourer on farms and building sites when he can find work. Sir Godfrey apparently hated him and refused to have anything to do with his daughter after she took up with him. According to the woman I spoke to, he told Elizabeth he was writing her out of his will unless she dropped Benny.'

'So we have to count Elizabeth as a suspect,' Agatha said, staring at her photograph. 'She looks remarkably like her mother, doesn't she? Gerald is also definitely a suspect. He was at loggerheads with his father over the signing of a will *and* the sale of the house to Freddy Evans.'

'I was talking to Edward when you got back,' Toni said. 'He found out that Gerald was also almost ready to lodge plans for a development on the property. He wants to restore Carseworth Manor and pay for it by building houses on some of the land, including the field where the fete was held.'

'But that land was gifted to the church,' Agatha pointed out.

'Gerald is a lawyer,' Toni said, 'and he reckoned he could have the gift covenant revoked.'

'His father wouldn't have liked that.' Agatha shook her head. 'If Sir Godfrey was blocking Gerald's plans and also refusing to sign a will Gerald had drawn up, then Gerald had plenty of reasons to want his father dead. He's starting to look like our prime suspect. See what else you can dig up on him, Toni.'

Patrick and Simon walked into the office, Simon's face breaking into his widest grin.

'What's all this?' he quipped, looking at Agatha and Roy. 'A meeting of the United supporters' club?'

'You're not funny, Simon.' Agatha frowned at him. 'How are things going, Patrick?'

'Fine, we're getting things ready to set up our stand for the match on Wednesday night,' Patrick said, squinting at the noticeboard. 'Is that Freddy Evans?'

'It is – you know him?' Roy asked.

'I know of him,' Patrick replied. 'He's a real nasty piece of work. There are all sorts of stories about him, but the law's never managed to catch up with him. His son-in-law is one of the directors of Mircester United.'

'Excellent!' Agatha announced brightly.

'Excellent?' Roy sounded worried. 'What's excellent about it?'

114

'It gives us his connection to this area,' Agatha explained. 'It's also how he knew about Sir Godfrey's death before you did. He must have been furious at the thought you weren't keeping your finger on the pulse up here.'

'What if that really was his car we saw?' Roy sounded worried. 'What if he's come here looking for me?'

'This isn't really his turf,' Patrick pointed out. 'That's probably one of the reasons he wanted you to deal with Sir Godfrey. He wouldn't want any of our home-grown villains thinking that he was muscling in on what they see as their territory.'

'There you have it, Roy,' Agatha said. 'Freddy Evans won't show his face around here because he doesn't want to start a turf war – always bad for business. Now, we need to talk to the Ancombe Archers and I'm not setting foot in public dressed like this, so you can toodle off to the car park and pick up my car. Then we can both go home to change before we track down Robin Hood.'

'Now you sound like the Sheriff of Nottingham,' Roy said, accepting the car keys that Agatha was jangling in front of him.

'Not at all,' Agatha said, wandering into her office. 'We're the good guys, remember?'

In Comfrey Maga, Benny Lambert slumped into a chair at the table in his kitchen.

'I think I gone and made things worse for us, Liz,' he said, staring at the mug of coffee Elizabeth had just put in front of him. 'But he was out to grab you and I can't have that.'

'Of course you can't, Benny,' she said, soothingly. 'You're my knight in shining armour. You didn't make things worse by pushing him over. Not for us, anyway. My dear brother, however, is about to find out how bad things will get for him.'

'Now, I don't want you doing anything silly, Liz,' Benny chided her. 'We got enough problems on our plate already.'

'Don't worry, Benny,' she said in a soothing voice, smiling gently at him. 'I'll take care of our little problems, and hand Gerald a few of his own. He's been a very bad boy, and he's going to pay for it.'

It took Agatha a matter of moments to find a phone number for the Ancombe Archers. When her call was answered, she was surprised to hear not the booming tone of Robin Hood, but a vaguely familiar woman's voice.

'I was hoping to have a word with Robin Hood,' Agatha said. 'My name's Agatha Raisin.'

'He's not here at the moment, Mrs Raisin,' came the woman's voice. 'Can I help? It's Petula – his Maid Marion.'

'Ah, yes, Maid Marion,' Agatha said, laughing. 'I'm sure you can help. What I really want to do is to talk to someone a bit more about archery and, more specifically, the arrows you use.'

'I thought you might call. The police officer I spoke to wanted to know about all that as well – about the arrow that killed old Pride.'

'Yes, poor Sir Godfrey.'

'"Poor Sir Godfrey"?' Petula repeated, sounding less than sympathetic. 'He can rot in hell, if you ask me!'

'Er . . . who was the police officer you spoke to?' Agatha asked, trying to calm Petula.

'Glass, I think his name was.'

'Ah, yes,' Agatha said in a matter-of-fact way. 'I know Inspector Glass. He's a good man.'

'Not like that old swine Pride!'

'No, not like . . . I take it you knew Sir Godfrey.'

'I used to work at Carseworth.'

'I see,' Agatha said, hoping that she sounded like she understood. 'I've heard a thing or two about the way women were treated at Carseworth Manor.'

'"A thing or two"?' Petula seemed addicted to repeating phrases used by others. 'A thing or two doesn't even scratch the surface, Mrs Raisin, believe me.'

'I do believe you, Petula, and I really would like to hear all about it. Inspector Glass's boss isn't such a nice man and he thinks I had something to do with Sir Godfrey's murder. I need to find out all I can about what happened at Carseworth Manor in order to track down the real killer and clear my name.'

'That's why I said I thought you might call. I heard you were going to be looking into the murder. You best come see me, Mrs Raisin. I can tell you far more than just a thing or two about Carseworth.'

They agreed to meet the following morning at Ancombe Village Hall, which the archers used as their headquarters, and Agatha rang off. She plucked at the sleeve of her hoodie where the cheap fabric was starting to make her itch. Muttering to herself about not being able to bear wearing the thing much longer, she checked her watch. Where on earth had Roy got to? He should have been back with the car ages ago.

At that moment, Roy Silver was in a side street close to where Agatha parked her car, standing beside a black Jaguar and looking down into the mean eyes of Freddy Evans. Roy was not a particularly tall man, but Evans only came up to his chin. Behind Evans, however, was a mountain of a man who dwarfed them both.

'You know, Roy, I just couldn't believe my eyes when I spotted you walkin' along the street back there,' Evans said. 'I'd go so far as to say I was surprised . . . and I don't like surprises.'

'No, no . . . not surprises,' Roy stammered, gulping down a lungful of air. He hadn't taken a breath since the Jaguar had pulled up alongside him and Evans stepped out. Now he could feel his hands and knees start to tremble. 'I-I'm a tiny bit surprised to see you, too . . .'

'I bet you are, Roy. I bet I'm the last bloke you was thinkin' you'd see here in Mircester.' He grabbed a fistful of Roy's hoodie. 'What I want to know is, why are you poncin' around in this gear?'

'I c-can explain that . . . I think . . .'

'That's a very good idea, Roy. I think you should explain as well. I think there's a whole lot of things you need to explain. You need to explain why the Carseworth deal looks like it's gone down the toilet. You need to explain why you've done nothin' about gettin' Pride's son back on board . . . and you need to explain why it looks like you've been pryin' into my business.'

'But I haven't been . . . I mean, I don't know what you're talking about, honestly.'

'Well, to tell you the truth, Roy, this ain't really the time or place for you and me to have a natter, but we do need to have a nice long chat, so you'd better come along with us.' Evans released Roy's hoodie and stepped to the side. 'Show Mr Silver to the car, Danny.'

The giant stepped forward, reached out with his left hand and grabbed hold of the hoodie just where Evans had let go. Roy tried to push the hand away but Danny's right arm swung round and a fist the size of a wrecking ball slammed into the side of his head. He felt a wave of nausea and dizziness overwhelm him and, had Danny's left hand not been clamped to his chest, he knew his knees would have given way. Rather than falling, however, he could feel himself being half-lifted, half-dragged round to the back of the car. As if watching himself in slow motion, he saw a blur of blue and yellow when he was flung into the boot. The lid was slammed shut and everything went dark.

Chapter Six

The offices of Pride & Harkness were housed in an elegant Victorian building in the older part of Mircester city centre, less than half a mile from the Raisin Investigations office, on the other side of Mircester Abbey. Gerald Pride trotted down the stone steps outside the building, his briefcase in one hand, his mobile phone clamped to his ear with the other.

'Yes, I know I'd have it all sorted out by now, but things haven't gone entirely to plan, have they?' he said, his voice tight with irritation. There was a pause while he listened to the response, crossing the narrow street to where his car was parked in a private bay.

'Okay, calm down,' he said, opening the door and throwing his briefcase onto the passenger seat. 'I'll be there in a few minutes.'

As he pulled out of the parking bay and drove off along the cobbled street, another car fell in behind him. The second car followed him, sometimes just a few car lengths behind, sometimes with a couple of cars between them. They travelled out of town through an area of low-rent shops selling the sort of second-hand sofas and scruffy appliances with which unscrupulous landlords furnished over-priced rental flats.

Before long, Gerald turned right onto a road that led into a small, neat estate of fairly modern, modest, semi-detached houses. He parked in the short driveway of one of the houses and a dark-haired woman met him at the front door. They embraced, kissed and went inside.

The driver of the second car, Toni Gilmour, took one last photo, then reached across to place her camera safely on the floor in the passenger footwell.

As if he didn't have enough to deal with, she thought to herself, Gerald Pride is carrying on with another woman. That's yet another mark against our prime suspect.

She considered whether to wait for him to emerge, then decided that she had enough with the photographs. The most important thing now was to find out who the woman was. It was a little late to go back to the office, so she turned the car to head for home.

Agatha sat in her office, drumming her fingers on her desk and listening, for the fourth time, to a message saying that Roy Silver's phone was unavailable. Why had he switched off his phone again? What was taking him so long? Where the hell was he? She hung up, jumped to her feet and stomped out into the main office.

'Where's Toni?' she asked, scanning the desks. Patrick and Simon looked up from their computer screens.

'She went out to see what she could dig up on Gerald Pride,' Simon said. 'Helen left to go home a few minutes ago.' He looked up at the clock on the wall, showing well after five-thirty.

'Roy hasn't come back yet,' she said. 'I'm a bit concerned.'

'I'm sure there's nothing to worry about,' Patrick said. 'He's probably snarled up in traffic.'

'But it's only minutes from here to where I park,' Agatha said. 'He should be back by now and he's not answering his phone. I need you to go look for him.'

'Could be someone blocked him in at the car park,' Patrick said, getting to his feet.

'Yeah,' Simon said, grabbing his leather jacket from the back of his chair. 'He might not have a phone signal down where you park. Don't worry, boss, we'll find him.'

'You should split up,' Agatha instructed them. 'Take different routes, cover all the streets between here and the car park. I'll stay here in case he comes back.'

Less than half an hour later, Patrick and Simon were back in the office, and there was still no sign of Roy.

'Wherever he's gone,' Simon said, 'he didn't take your car. It's right where you left it this morning.'

'Something's wrong,' Agatha said, sounding grim. 'I'm going to call the police.'

'They won't do anything,' Simon pointed out. 'Roy's not a child or a vulnerable person and he's not been missing for very long.'

'They will still log the report, though,' Patrick advised, lowering his lanky frame back into his office chair.

'I meant I would call John or Bill.' Agatha frowned, turning towards her office. 'At least they'll be able to tell us if there's been any kind of incident.'

'Er, boss . . .' Simon said, hesitantly, waggling his phone. 'I arranged to see a girl at the pub . . . I can call her and cancel if you want me here.'

'No, Simon.' Agatha rolled her eyes. 'Whatever Roy's up to, we can't let it interfere with your love life. Don't let the girl down – off you go.'

'I'll hang on here with you,' said Patrick, nodding goodbye to Simon, whose footsteps could immediately be heard skipping downstairs to the street door. A moment later, the footsteps were thundering back up again.

'Boss! Patrick! Quick – call an ambulance!' Simon yelled. 'Roy's lying on the pavement outside! He's hurt bad!'

They rushed downstairs, Patrick calling for an ambulance on the way. Roy lay on the ground beside the entrance to Raisin Investigations. His face was puffy and red, the swelling having closed his right eye completely. There was blood around his nose and mouth.

'Roy!' Agatha knelt beside him. 'Roy, can you hear me?'

His left eye focused on her for a moment and he raised his head, trying to speak. Simon folded his jacket, tucking it under Roy's head.

'Don't try to move, mate,' he said, softly. 'There's an ambulance on its way.'

Roy began mumbling again, and Agatha held his hand.

'Don't try to talk, either, Roy,' she said. 'Help will be here in no time.'

'How is he?' asked Mr Tinkler, appearing from his shop. 'I've called for an ambulance.'

Patrick nodded to confirm that an ambulance was already en route.

'What happened, Mr Tinkler?' Agatha asked, looking up at the old antiques dealer. 'Did you see who did this?'

'No,' Mr Tinkler replied, clearly deeply shocked. 'I heard a screech of car tyres, took a look outside to see what was going on and found him lying there. Then I rushed back in to call an ambulance. Do you think he'll be all right?'

'He's had a real pounding,' Patrick said, taking Roy's other hand to feel his wrist, 'but he's breathing and there's a strong pulse.'

The lane was suddenly filled with flickering blue light and a siren squawked. Agatha watched the ambulance pull up and two paramedics in green overalls hurried over to them. One was a young man, the other a slightly older woman.

'What happened here?' the woman asked, Patrick making space for her to kneel beside Roy.

'He's been beaten up and dumped on the pavement,' Patrick said. 'His name is Roy Silver.'

'Hello, Roy, my name's Denise. Can you hear me, Roy?' the woman asked, calmly and clearly. Roy responded groggily, as before.

'He's going to be all right, isn't he?' Agatha asked, pleading with the paramedic. 'Please tell me he'll be all right . . .'

'Let them do their job, Agatha.' She felt a hand on her shoulder and looked up to see Bill Wong standing over her. She hadn't noticed a police car following the ambulance into the lane but two uniformed officers were now talking to Simon and Mr Tinkler, notebooks in their hands. Bill helped her to her feet.

'He's such a gentle man,' Agatha said, her lower lip trembling. 'He wouldn't hurt a fly.'

'I know,' Bill said. 'As soon as they're ready to move him, I'll take you to the hospital so you can be there for him.'

'Thank you, Bill,' she said, standing straight, holding her head high and wiping a tear from the corner of her eye. 'He needs me – I will be there for him . . . and I'll find out who did this. Whoever it was, they're going to pay!'

An hour later, Agatha was pounding along a corridor in Mircester General. It was a different corridor in a different part of the hospital from where she had visited James. The lighting was the same, the smell was the same, the doors lining the corridor with their glass panels and dark blinds were the same but . . . wait a minute! Who the hell was that?

She caught sight of herself in one of the door panes and her heart sank into her sports shoes. She was still wearing the awful Mircester United hoodie and sweatpants. How could she have gone out in public looking like this? She paused for a moment, briefly checking her lipstick, then turning a little to the left, a little to the right, examining what she was wearing. Actually, she thought, shifting the shoulders of the hoodie slightly, on someone as straight-up-and-down as Toni or Alice, this would just be a baggy mess but with my figure, at least I'm able to give it some shape. Given that I've no choice right now, it will have to do, but it's most definitely . . . temporary. She then tutted, scolding herself for being so shallow and easily distracted, before making off along the corridor.

By the time she reached the emergency ward where she'd been told Roy had been taken, Bill, having parked the car, had caught up with her. A nurse directed them to seats in an alcove off the corridor, asking them to wait there as the doctor had not yet finished examining Roy. Agatha and Bill had exchanged only a few words on the short drive to the hospital. Now he was full of questions.

'Was Roy out on a job for you when this happened?' he asked.

'Sort of,' she answered. 'I'd sent him to bring my car round to the office.'

'What I meant was,' Bill went on, 'was Roy working with you on one of your cases? You see, he was dumped outside your office deliberately. He wasn't robbed – he still had his wallet, his phone, his watch and your car keys – and muggers don't deliver their victims back to their friends. He wasn't left on the street, he was brought back to your office. That seems to me like someone delivering a message to you. So was he working with you?'

'In a way,' Agatha explained. 'It's all tied up with the murder of Sir Godfrey Pride. Roy was already dealing with Sir Godfrey before I got involved.'

'How did he know Sir Godfrey?'

'He was acting on behalf of a London businessman,' Agatha said, wondering if she should give Bill the full story. He was a trusted friend, but she couldn't be sure if telling Bill about Freddy Evans would help, or simply make things more complicated. 'His client wanted to buy Carseworth Manor and turn it into a spa hotel, but the deal fell through.'

'Who is the London businessman?'

'Bill, I don't think Roy would want me to . . .' Agatha began, then decided that Bill would be able to find out about Freddy Evans himself anyway, so why hold back? 'Freddy Evans is his name.'

'I've heard of him,' Bill said. 'He's a very dodgy character. Is he behind what happened to Roy?'

'Probably – Roy was convinced Evans was going to punish him for not tying up the Carseworth deal.'

'Agatha,' Bill said slowly, shaking his head, 'you've got to leave Evans to us. If he's behind this, we'll get him.'

'Bill,' Agatha said with a sigh, 'I know you mean well, and I'm sure you truly believe you can nail Evans, but from what I hear, he stays one step ahead of the law. You can bet he'll have a cast-iron alibi covering him from lunchtime to midnight and beyond – with a dozen witnesses willing to back him up.'

'That's all very well, but I don't want you to end up in here like Roy, and . . .' He paused, suddenly realising what she was wearing, and plucked at the sleeve of her hoodie. 'When did you and Roy become United supporters?'

'It's temporary!' Agatha growled, slapping his hand away, then jumping to her feet when she saw a doctor approaching.

'Are you Mrs Raisin?' the doctor asked, looking up from her clipboard of notes to view Agatha through large spectacles with heavy black frames.

'Yes, that's me,' Agatha said. 'Is he going to be okay, doctor?'

'You're Mr Silver's next of kin?'

'Yes.'

Bill gave her a look of surprise.

'The paramedics needed to put someone's name on their form,' she explained quickly. 'So how is he doing, doctor? Can I see him?'

'He's sleeping now, and that's the best thing for him at the moment, so it would be good if you could come back tomorrow. Someone really put Mr Silver through the mill. He's suffering from concussion, so we're going to monitor his condition carefully through the night. He has three cracked ribs and extensive bruising to his face. I think he's lucky not to have had his cheekbone broken and he has a number of loose teeth, although they'll probably stabilise of their own accord in due course.

'It will take him a while to get over this, but he should make a full recovery. At first, I thought he'd been in a fight, but there are no wounds on his hands to indicate that he fought back. There were, however, these marks.'

She showed Agatha and Bill photographs on her phone of red weals around Roy's wrists.

'Snakes and bastards! They tied him up!' Agatha hissed, then stared off towards the room where Roy lay sleeping. 'Oh, Roy . . . you must have been terrified . . .'

'He's safe now, Mrs Raisin,' the doctor assured her. 'We'll look after him.'

'Come on, Agatha,' Bill said. 'Let me take you home.'

'No, not home,' Agatha said, quietly. 'Back to my car, please, Bill. I'll need it in the morning to get here to see Roy.'

On the drive home, Agatha talked to Patrick and he promised to let Simon and Toni know how Roy was doing. By the time she parked outside her cottage in Lilac Lane, the sky to the west was glowing orange, sending sunset streaks of pink and red to colour the clouds over Carsely. She had fed the cats and fished her last frozen lasagne out of the freezer when the doorbell rang. Squinting through the peephole, she saw John Glass standing on the doorstep.

'Hi.' He smiled when she flung open the door. 'I heard you'd had a really bad Monday and—'

She flung her arms round his neck and sobbed into his chest.

'You should have seen him, John!' she cried, sucking in air between the words. 'You should have seen what they did to him!' Then she stepped back, grabbed a tissue from the hall stand and wiped the tears from her face. When she looked at him again, there was dark determination in her eyes. 'Well, they're not going to get away with it. I'll get them for this!'

'If you're talking about Freddy Evans,' John said, following her into the house, 'you are not to go after him.'

'I can do whatever I . . .' Agatha could feel a surge of anger building. Nobody could tell her what to do, not even John, but she hesitated when he put his hands gently on her shoulders.

'You are not to go after him – not without me. I need to know you're safe. I need to *keep* you safe, so you're not to go after him without me.'

'Oh, John,' she said, taking a deep breath. 'I know you mean well but you have to think about your own career and Wilkes and . . .'

'I've been dealing with Wilkes for years – too many years. You leave him to me. Evans, on the other hand, we will bring down together.'

'If you're caught helping me . . .'

'I won't be. I'll keep you up to speed with the police operation from the inside and you can let me know what you come up with. We'll work as a team, keeping in step – like dance partners.'

She smiled and hugged him close. He leaned down and kissed her.

'Partners,' she said softly. 'Sounds good to me.'

'I'm glad . . . but now I have to get back to work. Let's talk around lunchtime tomorrow.'

She stood on tiptoes to kiss him again, watched him disappear down her garden path into the gathering darkness, then went back to her frozen lasagne.

The following morning, Agatha woke early, feeling bright and perky. Boswell and Hodge, curled up together at the foot of her bed, gave her wide-eyed looks of utter horror when she flicked the bedside radio alarm to a cheerful breakfast show playing lively pop music. The cats were used to a far more sedate start to the day. She met their scorn with a smile, tickling their ears.

What had put her in such a good mood, she wondered? Was it that she knew Roy was going to be all right? Was it that she'd had just one glass of wine with her evening meal rather than the bottle she and Roy would have polished off? Or was it because the wonderful Detective Inspector John Glass had promised to put his job on the line to be her 'partner'? Whatever it was, she decided to keep the feeling going all day, turning up the music so she could still hear it in the shower.

She put together a few essentials to take to Roy – pyjamas, toothbrush, the paperback book from his bedside – and trotted downstairs for her morning coffee. Tempted by the thought of breakfast, the cats raced after her. The morning sky was clear and blue, the temperature mild, yet the air had lost the soft fullness of summer. Autumn was now barely able to sheathe the sharp claws of winter. She stood in her back garden, cradling her coffee cup and planning her day. She would visit James at the hospital once she had seen Roy, then detour to Ancombe for a chat with Robin Hood and Petula before heading to the office.

Finishing her coffee, she stepped back into the kitchen and locked up, nodding her approval at the satisfying clunk of her high-security door locks. Before setting the alarm, she checked herself in the hall mirror, smoothing her hair and repairing her lipstick. She was wearing a dark green skirt with a short matching jacket and a white silk blouse. It wasn't her favourite outfit, but it had drawn a couple of unsolicited compliments last time she had worn it, so she was prepared to give it another airing. Two minutes later, she was pulling out of Carsely in the direction of Mircester.

At the hospital, she met the young doctor she had spoken to the previous evening. She looked weary, the tiredness making her seem smaller, as though she had shrunk during the night.

'Good morning!' Agatha gave her a cheerful greeting. 'How is our patient today?'

'Mr Silver is doing really well,' said the doctor, stifling a yawn. 'He's awake and he's been able to manage a little breakfast. Don't stay too long. What he really needs is rest.'

'Have you been working through the night? You must be exhausted.'

'It's been a long shift.' The doctor smiled. She took off her glasses and seemed to notice Agatha for the first time. 'That's a very nice outfit,' she said. 'I have a jacket a bit like that, but the colour suits you better.'

'You're very kind,' Agatha said, smiling. 'It's an old favourite.'

And from that moment on, it was.

Roy was sitting up in bed watching TV when Agatha walked into his room. She was shocked at the way the bruising around his face had darkened, looking even worse than it had the previous evening, but he smiled when he saw her, waving her closer and switching off the TV news.

'How are you feeling?' Agatha asked.

'Pretty sore – I ache absolutely everywhere, darling,' he said, 'but they're taking good care of me here.'

'I brought a few things I thought you might need,' she said, holding up the small overnight bag and taking a seat at his bedside. 'Oh, Roy, your poor face looks so swollen. Who did this to you?'

'I've already been through it all with Bill Wong. He was here earlier. The truth is, I don't remember much about it. I remember seeing blue and yellow – that dreadful hoodie and sweatpants – but the two things that stick in my mind most are the black Jaguar and Freddy Evans's mean little eyes.'

'So it was him – Evans.'

'Without a doubt.'

'If they abducted you when you were on your way to pick up my car, they must have plucked you off the street and taken you somewhere. Any idea where?'

'Not a clue, sweetie, but I remember those eyes. It was him.'

'I'll get him, Roy. I promise you, I'll get him for this.'

'Leave it to Bill and his boys, Agatha,' Roy said, reaching out to take her hand. 'The police can handle it. I don't want you getting into trouble.'

'Don't worry about me. I have my own kind of police protection now – and I'm working on a plan to deal with Evans. He'll get what's coming to him, but you mustn't think about all that any more. You need to concentrate on getting well, then you can recuperate at home with me in Carsely. You can stay as long as you like.'

133

They chatted for a while longer about Agatha's life in Carsely, how Roy planned on taking a long holiday once he was better and where he might go. Agatha then promised to let Tamara Montgomery know that her star riding pupil was in hospital before leaving to visit James. She was congratulating herself on having navigated the labyrinth of corridors between Roy's room and James's room when a male nurse caught her attention just before she opened James's door.

'It's Mrs Raisin, isn't it?' he said, waving to her. 'Mr Lacey asked me to keep an eye out for you. He's not in that room, you see.'

'Where is he?' Agatha asked, feeling slightly alarmed. 'Has something happened?'

'No, no, nothing like that,' the nurse said with a reassuring smile. 'He's doing very well and we moved him onto one of the wards so that we could use that room for another patient. Mr Lacey is just through here.'

He beckoned Agatha to follow him round a corner to where the corridor opened out onto a space where a dozen beds were arranged, six each side of a wide central aisle leading to a window that covered the full width of the far wall. Each of the beds had a curtain arrangement for privacy but all of the curtains were drawn back, revealing that every bed had a male occupant. She scanned the beds quickly, taking in each of the faces. Their ages ranged from what looked like mid-forties to anything approaching a century. Three appeared to be dozing and four were definitely sound asleep, two of them snoring loud enough to achieve an occasional turbulent harmony that made the hairs on the back of her neck prickle. It was a duet more evocative of a farmyard than a medical facility.

'Mr Lacey is the last bed on the right,' the nurse informed her.

Agatha made her way towards the window and the bed with the only face she hadn't scrutinised, mainly because James was sitting up, concealed behind that morning's *Daily Telegraph*. Two of the other men were watching a TV mounted high in the corner of the room, one was reading a book and the other – the youngest in the room – was sitting up with his arms folded, grinning broadly. He gave her a wink as she walked past and she was acutely aware that her presence had also caught the attention of the others. A flesh-creeping tingle wormed its way up her spine. They were watching her. She grew increasingly annoyed that she was allowing them to make her feel uncomfortable. Clearly, they had nothing better to occupy their minds than ogling the first female visitor of the day. By the time she reached James's bed, she was fairly sure she had been completely undressed in the minds of the four men. Did they expect her to feel flattered by their attention? No, they were simply gawking because they thought they could get away with it. On reaching the window, she turned to see them looking directly at her. She returned their stares with a scowl of defiance, blew them all a kiss and rolled her eyes to let them know how pathetic they were. Three of them immediately looked away in embarrassment and the winker burst out laughing.

'Agatha, how lovely to see you again!' Distracted by the laughter, James emerged from behind the broadsheet and folded the newspaper with military precision in half, in half again, then laid it on his lap. 'It's really good of you to come for another visit. I so hoped that you would, my dear.'

He reached for her hand, guiding her into the chair by his bed.

'Actually, poor Roy's ended up in here, too,' she explained, 'so this is a kind of double visit.'

James responded with a note of concern for Roy, the polite thing to do, Agatha thought, given that they had never been the best of friends. She assured James that Roy was going to be fine and he gave an enthusiastic smile.

'Good, I'm so glad,' he said, impressing Agatha with a show of energy and vigour that was in stark contrast to the weariness she had witnessed in him only the day before. 'I'm getting out of this confounded place tomorrow, and not a moment too soon. They're desperate for the beds, you know. The whole health system is collapsing and the people who work here are run off their feet. It's a question of logistics and the effective deployment of manpower. If you ask me, what they should do is—'

'James,' Agatha said, gently shaking her head to show her reluctance at the thought of listening to a lecture about how James's years of military experience could be brought to bear on the deficiencies of the National Health Service. 'It's good to hear you sounding off. You're clearly so much better than you were yesterday.'

'Indeed I am,' James agreed. 'Pretty much fighting fit again now that they've got the medication spot on. So I've been thinking – you do a lot of that in here – I'll admit to having a bit of a scare with the old tumour thing and that starts to make you realise that, well, life's too short. Too short for regrets. I think we should plan a trip as soon as I get out of here, my dear. Let's jet off somewhere for a spot of winter sunshine. Blow away the cobwebs, shake off past mistakes and start all over again. What do you say?'

'James, I . . .' Agatha cast her eyes around the ward. The winker was nodding, urging her to say yes. The reader had an eyebrow raised and his mouth turned down at the corners – definitely a 'no'. The other two had gone back to watching breakfast TV. So the room was split, and so was she. She looked back at James. 'There are a few too many eavesdroppers here for my liking,' she whispered. 'Let's talk about this when you get home. We can make proper plans then.'

She leaned forward, kissed him on the forehead and took her leave. As she walked past the winker, he sneered at her.

'You should have jumped at that offer,' he said.

'Not that it's any of your business,' Agatha said with a slight frown, 'but what makes you think that?'

'Well, it's obvious, isn't it?' he smirked. 'Chances like that aren't going to come along every day for a woman your age.'

'For a woman my . . .?' Agatha froze for an instant, then her head tilted slightly to one side and her jaw hardened, her mouth set in what some might have mistaken for a smile. 'And what is it that you're in for?' she asked, snatching the clipboard of notes hanging at the foot of his bed. 'Personality transplant, is it? Ooh, dear me, I don't like the look of that.' She flicked through the sheets of notes. 'You've got a lot of medication coming up – some really major, heavy-duty suppositories. Still, that shouldn't be a problem for an arse like you.'

She hung the clipboard back in place and stalked off. Leaving the ward, she glanced back to see the winker out of bed, frantically studying his notes, muttering, 'Suppositories? Nobody told me . . . Where does it say that . . .?'

In good time for her meeting in Ancombe, Agatha drove with no urgency, taking in the views where trees and hedgerows had begun dropping their leaves to reveal wide expanses of countryside. Farmers working their fields with tractors and combines confirmed that the harvest season was in full swing, and she caught a whiff of the dry, earthy scent drifting off the land. Agatha suddenly thought of Charles. He had once explained to her, on a ramble across his estate during a gloriously long, golden autumn weekend, that the word 'harvest' came from an Old English word meaning 'autumn'. Funny how things like that suddenly popped into your mind. Funny how a smell, a view or a word could bring back vivid memories of people and places – old friends and old lovers.

Pulling over into a convenient layby, she got out of the car and leaned against the front wing, staring out over the landscape. Charles was always there, always lurking in the background of her mind. She liked to fool herself into thinking that she couldn't care less about him any more but, if she was honest with herself, she knew that wasn't true. He still mattered. He was still part of her life and he always would be – but what about James? She breathed in the fresh country air and gave a short laugh. Not so long ago, at times like this, when she had thoughts to mull over, she'd have been sucking in cigarette smoke for a nicotine hit, but she'd knocked that habit on the head. Stopping smoking hadn't been easy, but when was anything ever easy? Living next door to James wasn't always easy, but she couldn't imagine him not being there. Unfortunately, neither could she imagine enjoying a romantic break somewhere with him.

The problem with James was that he started off with the best intentions, but then fell back into the habits of a lifetime. He was used to travelling on a shoestring budget and never gave a thought to all the comforts and little luxuries that she so enjoyed. To James a hotel room was simply somewhere to sleep. A large, well-appointed hotel room with a sumptuous bathroom was just a waste of money. Using a 'money-off' voucher in a restaurant was second nature to him, while she preferred to dine in places where presenting vouchers or coupons was entirely inappropriate. She'd have to find a way to let him down gently, given what he'd just been through. It would be difficult, but the same phrase sprang to mind once more – when was anything ever easy? Instinctively, she made to drop her cigarette butt and grind it under her shoe, then laughed again when she looked down at her empty hand.

Easing herself back into the car, she laid Charles and James to rest in her head with thoughts of John. She had grown very fond of him. Their relationship had built slowly rather than launching like a champagne cork but it had lasted the course, not fizzling out like the bubbles in sparkling wine. He was very special to her and he danced divinely, but was she in love with him? Were they to be long-term partners as well as dance partners? Time would tell, but for now they had the murder of Sir Godfrey Pride and the downfall of Freddy Evans to choreograph. She needed to get her mind back on the job.

The village of Ancombe was Carsely's closest neighbour and as postcard-perfect a Cotswold village as you could ever hope to find, the thatched roofs of its cottages as precisely manicured as the impeccably tended front gardens. Although smaller than Carsely, it attracted walkers and tourists in a way that Carsely, only slightly less attractive but more of a well-kept secret, did not. Ancombe's pub, the Feathers, served food to a standard that put the Red Lion to shame and the Ancombe Ladies Society regularly socialised with its Carsely equivalent. Those meetings often took place in Ancombe's village hall, which stood adjacent to the ancient church in the middle of the village.

The flock of tourists that descended on the area during the spring and summer months had begun to dwindle but there were still enough visitors around to make Agatha glad to find a parking spot right outside the church. The entrance to the village hall was off to the right and she found the door standing open. When she ventured inside, she immediately spotted Robin Hood tucking documents and pamphlets into a satchel. He looked up when she called 'Good morning,' grinned and welcomed her to what he described as 'Robin Hood's lair!'

'You look like you're about to set off somewhere,' she said.

'That I am,' he agreed. 'I am lucky enough to be retired and able to devote much of my time to the Archers. We are constantly seeking out new sponsors, of course, and I have a meeting in Evesham a little later this morning to raise funds. Robbing from the rich to give to the poor – it's Robin Hood's way, after all! Now, how can I help you?'

'You know that I've become mixed up in the murder of Sir Godfrey Pride?'

'Yes, terrible business – simply terrible. I suppose you know that he founded the Ancombe Archers? I was talking to him only that morning. I hear you found the body. That must have been awful for you.'

'Yes, yes, it was,' Agatha said, resisting the temptation to point out that it wasn't the first corpse she'd had to deal with. Robin's sympathy would help to keep him on her side. 'That's partly why I want to find out more about what actually happened.'

'The police spent a great deal of time with me on Saturday,' Robin said, 'and they've been in touch several times since – lots of questions.'

'Could you bear to answer a few for me?' Agatha asked, pleading with her eyes. 'He was killed with an arrow, you see, and I need to know how that could have happened.'

'I can assure you that it wasn't one of our arrows. Every one fired at the fete was accounted for.'

'I had no doubt they would be, but someone fired the thing at him. It might help to know, for example, how far away an archer could be and still kill a man?'

'That would all depend on what kind of bow was being used and its draw weight, but a bow is most certainly a deadly weapon even at long range. When English and Welsh archers used their longbows against the French army at Crécy in 1346, they were lethally accurate at up to three hundred metres. Nearly seven centuries later, modern bows are just as accurate, even in the hands of less well-schooled archers.'

'I see. Where do you get the arrows you use?'

'We use various suppliers, but all of the archery equipment we use can be bought at specialist sports stores and, of course, absolutely everything is available on the internet. Let's take a look at some of our stuff – Petula's in the store room now.'

He led the way to the back of the hall, calling out to Petula, who appeared from a doorway.

'Hello, Mrs Raisin,' she said brightly. 'We've been expecting you. Come in and I'll show you the kit.'

Agatha noted the heavy metal locks on the store-room door and followed Petula inside where the walls of the long, windowless room were lined with different types of bow in custom-made racks and shelves with neatly stowed quivers and protective gear. There were stacks of straw targets on the floor along with tall, round wicker baskets, each filled with different kinds of arrow. There was a wooden work table in the middle of the room.

'These are the arrows we were using on Saturday,' Petula explained, selecting a couple. 'You probably recognise them.'

'I do,' said Agatha. 'They're the same as the one used to kill Sir Godfrey.'

'I'm not saying it couldn't be done,' Robin said, lifting one of the targets to stand it upright on the table, 'but hitting a moving target, in those woods, where trees would constantly be interfering with your line of sight, would be damned difficult.'

'Easier from close range, I should think,' Agatha commented.

'Most definitely,' Robin said, picking up an arrow to demonstrate. 'At short range, an arrow will fly straight and true.' He held the arrow level and touched its tip on the gold bullseye. 'At longer range, gravity and air resistance will have an effect and the arrow will start to drop.' He brought the arrow up to the target, letting the tip curve down to point at the lower part of the blue ring. 'To compensate for that, at very long range you would want to fire the arrow into the air, so that it travels in an arc.' He showed the arrow rising from a start point and curving to drop towards the target, holding the tip against the bulls-eye and the tail raised as though it had hit at a downward angle.

'Is it possible an arrow could lodge in the target like this?' Agatha asked, taking the arrow and showing it with the tail down, as though it had come from below.

'Anything's possible,' said Robin. 'I suppose it could have a bit of a wibble if it hit a downdraught of air or something, but it's highly unlikely it could ever come in at such an acute upward trajectory.'

Agatha stared at the arrow and fell silent, suddenly realising what had been troubling her about the macabre scene in the woods. It was the arrow. Sir Godfrey Pride had not been shot with an arrow at all. That part of the murder scene was a complete lie.

Chapter Seven

'Agatha, I really must be going now, I'm afraid,' Robin said, apologetically, 'but Petula will be able to answer any other questions you might have.'

'That I will,' Petula said, nodding to Agatha in a meaningful way.

'Yes . . . yes, of course. Thank you, Robin,' Agatha said, snapping her thoughts away from the scene in the woods and the image of the arrow embedded in Sir Godfrey's chest, back to the present. 'You've been most helpful.'

Once he was gone, Petula replaced the target on the stack and dropped the arrow back into the correct basket while talking to Agatha.

'We're all volunteers here,' she explained. 'The Ancombe Archers is a charity and those of us who help out give what time we can to keep the club going. I always like to make sure everything is neat and tidy here in our store room.'

'Does the club still work with disadvantaged youngsters?' Agatha asked.

'Very much so,' Petula explained. 'That's what old man Pride set it up for, and that's what we've continued to do, although he didn't do much for us over the past few years. His son and daughter still help out, though. We don't see so much of Gerald here, but Elizabeth and her partner, Benny, are still involved. I'm guessing it's not them you want to talk about, though – it's *him* and Carseworth.'

'You guess right. You said you could tell me all about what went on at the manor.'

'Take a seat, Mrs Raisin,' Petula said, dragging two folding chairs out from under the table. 'I'm not sure exactly how much you already know.'

'Not a great deal,' Agatha explained. 'How many people worked there, for instance?'

'Usually three when I was there. There had been four in the past. I worked as a maid and cleaner – general dogsbody, really. There was also a cook and a gardener, although she only did three days a week. Most didn't stay too long. Over the years, I can think of around twenty who were there at one time or another.'

'And did Sir Godfrey always treat you all like his personal playthings?'

'He was worse with some than others, especially when he really turned to the drink. I'm told things weren't so bad when his wife was alive. I never met her but I know some of the girls who worked there complained to her and she told them that her husband was "a bit of a rascal" and that they should just ignore him.'

'You mean she didn't object to him groping these young women?'

'She seemed to think it was all just a bit of fun.'

146

'A bit of fun?' Agatha could scarcely believe that any woman would put up with her husband abusing their female employees. 'She didn't think what he was doing was a disgrace?'

'She dismissed it as high spirits. I don't suppose things were any different in the house where she was brought up. Anyway, the old man really went from bad to worse when she died. Even when times were hard and jobs were scarce, people saw Carseworth Manor as a last resort. There was one girl, though, who put up with him longer than most – Carol Hendricks. She was there for years. I remember she had a real reputation with the boys. She was nice enough to talk to but always said she "liked to live life to the full". Yet even she walked out in the end. Rumour was that she was pregnant and he sacked her.'

'The child was Sir Godfrey's?'

'Unlikely – the girls never let each other be caught alone with him. Anyway, I don't think he would have gone so far as to have sex with any of us. He was just a very sad man who got a thrill out of touching young women. He certainly didn't want anything to do with anyone who was pregnant.'

'So who was the father?'

'Carol never said, even to the day she died. Lung cancer took her in the end, poor girl.'

'What happened to the child?'

'He was raised by his grandmother and turned out a complete slimeball. You've met him – Peter Hendricks – Spider.'

'And no one owned up to being his father?'

'Not as far as I know. Carol had plenty of boyfriends. She never settled down with any of them. Very independent. She was devoted to her little boy, though. It wasn't until she died and he was left with his grandmother that he started to go off the rails.'

'And he's one of your Ancombe Archers.'

'Yes, he is.' Petula gave a sharp, humourless laugh. 'Robin still believes the Archers should stick to their principles and we are still here to help youngsters who need it. Spider has been one of us for a good few years. The Archers have been the one constant thing in his life. He's been with us far longer than he's been with that girlfriend of his.'

'I understand that she used to work at Carseworth, too.'

'She was the last of them – Amy Cobb. She's pregnant, you know. They say the old man sacked her when he found out, just like he sacked Spider's mum.'

'You can't sack a woman for being pregnant!'

'He did whatever he liked. He paid cash-in-hand and most who worked there were grateful for it, until they got sick of the old man, or he was too broke to pay their wages. Amy would certainly have needed the money with a baby on the way. I reckon if anyone was to hold a grudge against Pride it would be her.'

'You could be right,' Agatha agreed, mentally adding Spider and Amy to her list of suspects, then scowling, appalled at the thought of what went on in Sir Godfrey Pride's house. 'Carseworth Manor sounds like a nightmare! I mean, lots of women have to cope with some degree of unwelcome attention from a colleague or a boss, and there are ways – official and unofficial – to deal with it, but Sir Godfrey Pride's behaviour tops the lot. Do you think he might have been the father of Amy Cobb's baby?'

'Even more unlikely than Carol's. He was so drunk most of the time these past few years that he could hardly stand up – in every sense, I reckon, if you get my meaning.'

'He sounds disgusting.' Agatha shook her head. 'How could you bear it? How long did you work for him?'

'A few months. I left as soon as I could find another job. That was about twenty years ago. Now I have my own little cleaning business – offices mainly.'

'Offices – yes, that's where I should be,' Agatha said, looking at her watch. 'Thank you for talking to me, Petula. You've been a great help.'

'My pleasure, Mrs Raisin. Feel free to call me any time.'

Agatha drove out of Ancombe heading for Mircester, mulling over everything she had learned from Petula. Spider's mother had got pregnant and been sacked. Could Spider actually be Sir Godfrey's son, despite what Petula said? He'd also sacked Amy when she got pregnant. Surely he couldn't have fathered a child with her, too? And yet . . . the note found on his body was signed 'A'. Could that be 'A' for Amy? Could she have lured the old man to the spot where he was murdered? Was she the murderer?

Then there was the arrow – that was something Agatha needed to go through with the team back at the office. She drove a little faster, flouting the speed limit until she was forced to slow in traffic on the outskirts of Mircester.

It was late morning when Agatha walked into the office to find Toni about to pin a few photos to the board, watched by Simon and Patrick. She perched on Simon's desk to see what Toni had come up with.

'It would appear,' Toni said, 'that Gerald Pride has a bit on the side. Sorry . . . I, um, didn't mean that to rhyme. I followed him last night to a house in the suburbs where he met with this woman.' She pinned up a photograph of Gerald embracing his lover. 'It looks very much like he's having an affair. This morning, I've been able to identify her as . . .'

'Petula!' Agatha's mouth dropped open. 'Good grief! I've just been talking to her! She's one of the Ancombe Archers!'

'Petula Grant,' Toni confirmed. 'She runs a cleaning business. One of her clients is Gerald's firm, Pride & Harkness.'

'She used to work at Carseworth Manor,' Agatha said. 'She'd have been there around the time that Gerald came home from university.'

'Maybe his old man wasn't the only one knocking off the staff,' offered Simon.

'Not quite how I would have put it,' Agatha said, glaring at Simon to show her disapproval of his vulgar turn of phrase, 'but like father, like son, as they say.'

'I doubt Gerald could have conducted an affair for all those years without anyone finding out, especially when he got married,' Patrick pointed out.

'Maybe it's been an on–off thing,' Toni suggested.

'An old flame rekindled from time to time,' said Agatha, Charles popping into her mind again. She gave her head a little shake to get rid of him. 'It happens, but it also means that Petula joins our list of suspects. Gerald could have been working with Petula just as he could have been plotting with Stephanie to murder his father.'

'What would Petula stand to gain from it?' asked Simon.

'Maybe Gerald promised her that he would ditch his wife and they would have a life together once he got hold of his father's property,' said Patrick.

'Exactly,' Toni agreed. 'Petula basically has the same motive as Stephanie. Get the old man out of the way so they can do as they please with Carseworth Manor.'

'Perhaps,' Agatha said, 'although Stephanie didn't want to live there, while Gerald did. If Gerald was planning to divorce her and move Petula into Carseworth, of course, Stephanie could simply be paid off with a divorce settlement. We also have two more suspects to add to our murder board.'

Agatha tore a sheet of paper from a notepad on Simon's desk, wrote two names on it and pinned it to the board.

'Spider and Amy?' said Toni.

'Peter Hendricks and his girlfriend Amy Cobb,' Agatha said. 'Petula told me that Amy is pregnant and that Sir Godfrey sacked her, just as he did in the past with Spider's mother.'

Toni sighed, shaking her head, Patrick frowned and even Simon seemed taken aback, his usual grin replaced by a look of stern disapproval.

'So Spider and Amy have good reason to hold a grudge against Sir Godfrey,' he said.

'There has to be more to it than that, though,' Patrick said. 'Could Pride have got Amy pregnant? Is it possible they were having an affair? She could be the "A" who signed the note.'

'She could be,' agreed Agatha, 'but it takes a certain kind of callous individual to write a note like that in order to lure an old man to his death. Toni, you and I need to have a chat with Amy Cobb. We need to know if she's really capable of premeditated murder.'

'I'll track down an address for her,' Toni said, nodding.

'In the meantime, I've something else to share with you,' Agatha said. 'It appears that almost anyone can buy a bow and a stock of arrows. Sir Godfrey Pride, however, was not *shot* with an arrow.'

Her announcement was met with puzzled stares.

'Stand up, Simon,' Agatha said, getting to her feet and taking a ruler from Simon's desk. She positioned him in front of the pin-board. 'An arrow fired from close range would have hit fairly straight.' She demonstrated with the ruler, holding it against Simon's chest, parallel to the ground, then changed it to a downward angle. 'From long range, it would most likely hit like this . . . but the arrow that killed Sir Godfrey came in like this . . .' Agatha drew back her arm and thrust the ruler swiftly upwards until it touched Simon's shirt.

'Somebody stabbed him with the arrow?' Toni said. 'Why would you do that?'

'To make it look like he'd been shot,' Patrick suggested. 'To try to blame an archer for the murder and throw all of us off the scent.'

'Maybe,' Agatha said, 'but an archer would know that hitting a moving target in the woods where there might not always be good line of sight could be a tricky shot. An archer would also know that an arrow is a deadly weapon, even if it's not fired from a bow, so we can't rule anyone out. I think the fact that the arrow was used to stab Sir Godfrey is one of the things that came to light in the pathologist's report Wilkes didn't want me to see.'

'So we can be fairly sure he was stabbed, not shot, maybe by someone who could handle a bow, maybe not,' Simon said, taking his ruler back from Agatha. 'How does that help us?'

'Every little detail that builds a picture of what happened in the woods that morning helps,' Agatha said, 'even if we don't yet understand exactly why. Anyone have anything else to add?'

They all shook their heads.

'All right,' Agatha said. 'Patrick, what are you and Simon up to today?'

'We have meetings with suppliers,' Patrick said, 'so that we have all the stock we need for the burger van.'

'I know it sounds a bit over the top,' Simon said when he saw Agatha raise an eyebrow, 'but we have to look like the real deal.'

'Of course,' Agatha said. 'Your cover needs to be water-tight. Toni, that leaves you and me to track down Spider and Amy, as well as trying to keep tabs on Mr Parsons. Today is one of his mysterious afternoons out, isn't it?'

Toni confirmed that Mrs Parsons had said her elderly husband was due to go missing again that afternoon, and Agatha declared the meeting over. They all went back to their desks and Agatha had no sooner settled into her office than Helen Freedman appeared with a stack of papers that required her attention, a cup of coffee and the offer of fetching Agatha a lunchtime sandwich. Agatha accepted all three, then began leafing through the paper-work with a distinct lack of enthusiasm. She knew that Helen made the admin chores as straightforward for her as she possibly could, but when all was said and done, chores were still chores. She was glad when, after a few minutes, her phone rang. She was even happier that it was John.

'I've come up with a couple of interesting things,' he said. 'In the pathologist's report . . .'

'Don't tell me,' Agatha interrupted him. 'He wasn't shot, he was stabbed.'

'Correct. You've been busy, haven't you? The forensics people couldn't get any prints off the arrow, but it was clear that it had been grasped around the shaft. They're running more tests on it tomorrow.

'The other thing is that Wilkes knows that Roy was working with you. He now believes that you were in on the deal to buy Carseworth Manor all along. As far as he's concerned, the murder is all tied up with Roy's deal and you're in the thick of it. He's waiting for the right moment to haul you back in for questioning.'

'Really?' Agatha groaned, resting her head on her free hand. 'That's all I need right now . . . mind you . . . on the other hand . . . Can we meet up for a proper chat later?'

'Sure. I've just come off shift and I want to get my head down for a couple of hours. Then I have an appointment I can't shift, but I'll be free late this afternoon.'

Agatha rang off just as Helen appeared with her sandwich. She unwrapped it eagerly, then eyed it with suspicion.

'It's chicken tikka with fresh salad and green chutney,' Helen said defensively. 'I'm sure you'll love it. I'll bring you a cup of tea.'

Agatha took a tentative bite, immediately realised it was delicious and, not having eaten since last night's frozen lasagne, had almost wolfed it all down by the time Helen returned with the tea. She thanked Helen profusely.

'You need to eat properly and regularly, Mrs Raisin,' Helen said, 'for brain power and to keep you in good shape.'

Agatha's secretary walked out of her office, head held high and shoulders back, pleased that her choice of sandwich had met with the boss's clear approval and that she had been able to deliver some sage advice.

Once she had finished her lunch and worked through her paperwork, Agatha grabbed her handbag, heading out into the main office.

'Did you track down Spider and Amy's address?' she asked Toni, walking over to Helen's desk with her papers.

'Yes, got it,' Toni said, grabbing her notebook and getting to her feet while draining a cup of something.

'What's that stuff?' Agatha asked, sniffing and wrinkling her nose.

'Instant soup-in-a-cup,' Toni responded. Agatha tutted.

'You need to eat properly and regularly, Toni,' she said, tapping her temple. 'For brain power and to keep in shape.' Agatha winked at Helen, who did her best to wink back but closed both eyes instead of just one and ended up looking like a startled kitten.

With Agatha driving, Toni directed them out of Mircester town centre and beyond the railway station. If ever there was a town where people could come from, or live on, 'the wrong side of the tracks', it was Mircester. To the east of the station lay rambling railway marshalling yards, overgrown with giant weeds and largely disused since freight took to the roads in giant articulated trucks. Brooding over the yards were dilapidated, sometimes even derelict buildings and shabby industrial units. Toni glanced down a side street past a seedy-looking pub called the Sportsman. The two men standing smoking outside looked far from athletic.

'Remember when we went into the strip club further down that street?' she said.

'Shirlie's Girlies,' Agatha replied. 'How could I forget?'

'The owner thought we were a double act,' Toni started laughing, 'then Wilkes came out of nowhere and arrested us!'

'All he did was embarrass himself, as usual.' Agatha grinned, shaking her head. 'Do you remember who was with him that day? Inspector John Glass. Who'd have thought he'd turn out to be one of the good guys?'

'Who'd have thought?' Toni repeated. 'And now you go dancing with him!'

'Not quite the sort of dancing we saw that day, though!'

They both laughed, and Toni pointed out a turning they needed to take.

'There aren't too many dull moments with you around,' she said. 'Life would be pretty flat without you.'

'Well, I'm not about to let any dull moments sneak up on you.' Agatha grinned. 'Just stick with me, Toni, and we'll keep life interesting. I'm not going anywhere.'

'Look up ahead.' Toni pointed at three figures beside a car. 'That's Spider.'

'And that's Gerald Pride's car,' Agatha added, pulling over to park. 'Grab a couple of photos before we get close, Toni. This may be another of those not-so-dull moments.'

Toni made sure she snapped all three of the people, then stowed the camera out of sight in the car before she and Agatha began to approach the group. Gerald Pride was standing with his back to his car, remonstrating with Spider and Amy outside a small block of rundown flats.

'Stay well clear of my office, you hear?' Gerald roared at them. 'Don't bother coming begging at my door ever again, because you're getting nothing!'

'We ain't beggars!' Spider shouted back. 'We just want what's rightfully ours! The old man owed us, so now you do, too!'

'I owe you nothing!' Gerald snarled, poking a finger just an inch from Spider's face. Spider slapped the hand away and Gerald swiftly swung it back, this time with his fist clenched. The punch connected with Spider's nose and the younger man staggered backwards, tripped and fell to the pavement.

'Stop it! Stop it, both of you!' Amy stepped between them, then crouched over Spider, helping him to his feet. At that moment, Gerald realised Agatha and Toni were standing by his car.

'Oh, not you as well!' he snarled. 'It's bad enough having to deal with this scum! I don't need you poking your nose in!'

'It's poor Spider who's had a poke in the nose,' Agatha said, stepping towards Spider and offering him a delicate lace-trimmed cotton hankie from her handbag to mop a dribble of blood running from his nose. 'Must be your weak spot, eh, Spider?'

'We ain't scum!' he barked, holding the hankie to his nose. 'We just want what's right!'

'You're scum,' Gerald growled. 'Scum and liars.' Throwing himself into his car, he started the engine and sped off.

'What was he talking about?' Agatha asked. 'What does he think you're lying about?'

'We ain't lying about nothing!' Spider muttered. He removed the hankie from his nose, dabbed it back again to check that the bleeding had stopped, then returned it to Agatha. To Toni's surprise, Agatha accepted the blood-ied hankie and tucked it carefully back into her handbag.

'So what did you want from him?' Toni asked. 'Compensation, perhaps, for Sir Godfrey sacking Amy?'

'Bugger compensation!' Spider yelled, pointing at Amy. 'They have to pay for that baby! She's carryin' the old man's child!'

'No . . . no . . .' Amy burst into tears, sinking to the ground. Spider moved towards her, as if to help, but Amy waved him away and he stood for a moment, staring at her with what Agatha suspected was a look of real concern.

'I need a beer,' he grumbled and, reverting to type, he spat blood on the ground before stomping into the building. Agatha and Toni knelt beside Amy.

'Are you all right?' Toni asked. 'Do you want us to call an ambulance?'

'I'm okay,' Amy said, sobbing. Toni handed her a tissue from a pocket pack.

'Not as nice as the hankie Agatha gave Spider, I'm afraid,' she smiled.

'Thank you,' Amy said, wiping the tears from her eyes. 'Would you help me up, please?'

Taking an arm each, Agatha and Toni helped the heavily pregnant Amy to her feet.

'Can we take you inside?' Toni offered.

'No, I'll be fine, honest,' Amy said.

'Spider wasn't being honest, though, was he?' Agatha said. 'The baby isn't Sir Godfrey's, is it?'

'Sir Godfrey is . . . I mean . . . when I worked at Carseworth . . .' Amy seemed unsure of herself.

'Take it easy, Amy,' Agatha said, gently. 'I could tell by the look on your face when you sat down on the pavement that you're tired of this charade. Sir Godfrey wasn't the father of your child, was he? It's Spider's baby, isn't it?'

'Yes, yes, it's his,' Amy said, with a heavy sigh. 'He wanted me to say it was Sir Godfrey's so that . . .' She paused, seemingly out of breath.

'So that he could screw some money out of the old man.' Agatha finished her sentence for her. 'When he died, Gerald was the one who had to pay up.'

'But I wouldn't . . . I mean . . . I never let that old man anywhere near me . . .' Amy took a deep breath and clutched her stomach and let out a squeal. Toni flung an arm around her and looked to Agatha.

'Agatha, fetch the car!' she ordered.

'Fetch the . . .? Who do you think you're . . .?'

'Fetch the car, Agatha! The baby's on its way!'

Agatha Raisin – who knew all about PR, who knew precisely how to run a successful business, who knew everything about being a private investigator – knew nothing about babies. She stood for an instant, stupefied, until Toni bellowed, 'Run! Now!' then turned and sprinted up the street faster than even she would have thought possible on four-inch heels. By the time she pulled alongside in the car, Spider had joined Toni and Amy. He helped them both into the back of the car before jumping into the passenger seat with, Agatha was pleased to note, a pale and worried expression.

'She'll be okay, won't she?' he kept repeating, reaching over to where Amy was sprawled against Toni and taking her hand. Amy was breathing heavily.

'She'll be fine, Spider,' Toni said, holding Amy safely in her arms, encouraging her to breathe steadily, telling her not to panic, assuring her everything was going to be fine.

Agatha concentrated on the road and the quickest route to Mircester General even though, by now, she knew her way to the hospital as well as she knew her way to Lilac Lane. At that moment in time, all things being equal, she would far rather have been heading home to Lilac Lane.

'How do you know so much about babies?' Agatha asked, sitting on yet another plastic chair in yet another corridor on yet another visit to the hospital.

'I helped deliver my cousin when I was twelve,' Toni replied, 'and there was pretty much always somebody we knew who was pregnant while I was growing up. There were always babies around.'

'I've never had much to do with them,' Agatha said. 'I'm not sure I'd have made a good mother. It's not for every woman, you know. I'm too self-centred, far too selfish.'

'Rubbish,' Toni said. 'You'd have been a great mum. You're always there for those you care about. We haven't always seen eye-to-eye on everything but I know for a fact I could count on you if I needed you.'

'You could,' Agatha said. 'I shouldn't like to think I'd ever let you down. Funny how Spider's attitude changed, wasn't it? In the car he was suddenly really worried about Amy.'

'It happens,' Toni said. 'Some men can ignore what's going on all the way through a woman's pregnancy and then, when it all starts happening, reality kicks in and they start to become fathers.'

'Let's hope the new Spider is a permanent version. Amy will need him now and—'

She was interrupted by the appearance of a nurse, who came towards them with a pleasant smile on her face.

'What's happened?' Agatha asked. 'Has the baby arrived?'

'No, not yet,' the nurse said. 'Both she and the baby are absolutely fine but this is her first child, so the delivery could take a few hours yet. Mr Hendricks is with her and he asked me to thank you both for bringing them in.'

'Would you give him this, please?' Agatha fished in her handbag and handed the nurse her business card. 'Ask him to let me know as soon as the baby's born.'

Toni glanced at Agatha's handbag before she closed it and saw a plastic evidence bag containing the bloodied hankie.

'Is that the hankie you gave Spider?' she asked. 'Why did you bag it like that?'

'It's a trick I've used before,' Agatha said, snapping the handbag shut. 'I may not know much about babies, but I do know how to find their fathers. Now,' she added, checking her watch, 'let's get going. We're still in time to tail the mysterious Mr Parsons.'

The Parsonses's house was a small bungalow in a cul-de-sac of identical buildings just off the road to Evesham. The houses were modern, with small front gardens and

space to park a modest car. They were the kind of properties where people spent their retirement years, having
downsized from larger homes where they brought up
their families.

Agatha drove into the cul-de-sac, confirmed that Mr
Parsons's car was still in his driveway, then drove back
out again, like a lost tourist. She was aware that net
curtains were twitching, that unseen eyes would be
watching.

'We'll park out on the main road,' she said. 'We can
pick him up when he leaves.'

They didn't have long to wait. Within a few minutes,
Mr Parsons's neat little hatchback nosed out of the cul-
de-sac and Agatha fell in behind him. They tailed him for
only a few minutes before he turned off the main road
into a suburban area of detached houses. Agatha had the
distinct feeling that she had been in the district before,
but couldn't quite place why.

'He's turning left up ahead,' Toni noted, taking a
couple of photographs, 'and pulling over in front of that
white house.'

'So I see,' Agatha said, 'but I know this place. Wait a
minute . . . I've only ever come here from the other direction. I know whose house that is!'

As if to confirm her assertion, John Glass appeared at
the front door to welcome Mr Parsons. Toni looked at
Agatha, mystified.

'What on earth's going on?' she said.

'That's what we're here to find out,' Agatha replied,
unclipping her seatbelt. 'Come on, let's sneak down the

side of the house and take a look around before we speak to John.'

They negotiated the small passage between the house wall and the garden fence, then paused to look out over the back garden. There were flower beds and a stretch of lawn on a shallow slope reaching down to the bottom of the garden where the ground flattened, and there was a large summerhouse with many windows. John and Mr Parsons were in the summerhouse. As soon as Agatha and Toni stepped onto the lawn, John spotted them, strolling out of the summerhouse to meet them, a broad grin on his face.

'Agatha!' he said, taking her hands and kissing her on the cheek. 'This is a surprise – and Toni, too! I have to say, you've got here just in time. I could use a little help, but what are you doing here?'

'We followed Mr Parsons,' Agatha explained. 'His wife's worried about him going off and coming home smelling of perfume.'

'Ah, that will be Gloria,' John said. 'She lives further along the street, but she can't make it today.'

'Make it for what?' Agatha demanded. 'What's Mr Parsons doing here?'

'Come inside,' he said. 'I'll show you.'

John introduced Agatha and Toni to George Parsons, who looked embarrassed, shifting uncomfortably from foot to foot when they shook hands. Agatha noted that he was wearing patent leather shoes, then cast her eyes around the summerhouse. The full-length windows and glass doors that made up the front wall were complemented by full-length mirrors on the back wall. The rest of the space was practically bare, apart from four speakers and a sound system.

'It's . . . a dance studio . . .' Agatha decided.

'That's right,' John said. 'A few years back, when my wife left me, I started building this as a hobby project. I'm particularly proud of the floor – took me ages to get it right, but it dances superbly.' He tapped a patent leather shoe on the wooden floor. 'From time to time, I give private dance lessons.'

'You're learning to dance, Mr Parsons?' asked Toni.

'Yes,' he said, smiling meekly. 'John has been teaching me. Gloria helps.'

'Well, it's never too late to learn something new,' Agatha said, 'but why dancing – why now?'

'For Judy – my wife,' he said. 'When we were married sixty years ago, I was a hopeless dancer – "two left feet" is what they used to say. When we had to take the floor at our wedding, dancing for the first time as man and wife, it was a disaster. I was so nervous and useless that I tripped and nearly fell flat on my face. But Judy was a strong lass. She kept me upright. Over the years, I've always managed to avoid dancing. Now, at our big diamond party, I want to do her proud. I want to waltz her round the dancefloor like I should have done all those years ago. It was to be a surprise.'

'I'm afraid the surprise has rather backfired,' Agatha said, then turned to Toni, who had a tissue in her hand, dabbing a tear from her eye.

'That's just so, so sweet,' was all she could say.

'Oh, pull yourself together,' Agatha said, slapping the car keys into her hand. 'Go pick up Mrs Parsons and bring her here. I think that's the best way to explain everything.'

Toni headed off up the lawn and Agatha took Mr Parsons by the hand, leading him to the middle of the floor.

'Come on, George,' she said. 'There's time for one last practice waltz before Judy gets here! Music, John!'

'Go on, George, you're ready for it,' John said, seeing the old man's slight hesitation. 'And Agatha's way better than Gloria.'

They were still gliding around the summerhouse under John's watchful eye, Mr Parsons growing in confidence with every word of encouragement from his teacher, when Toni led Mrs Parsons into the summerhouse. Agatha stopped and Mr Parsons thanked her before walking towards his wife with his hand outstretched.

'May I have this dance?' he asked.

'You old fool,' she said, smiling and shaking her head. 'Of course you can.'

They flitted off across the floor in perfect harmony, as though they had been dancing together for decades.

'We should leave them to it,' Agatha said. 'How about a cup of tea? I'm pretty sure they'll be needing one, too, before long.'

They walked up to the house where John busied himself in the kitchen.

'Any progress on the murder?' he asked, and Agatha brought him up to date.

'So we still have a full list of suspects – Gerald and Stephanie; Gerald and Petula; Freddy Evans; Spider and Amy; and Elizabeth and Benny.'

'Ah, yes, Pee-Bee,' said John.

'Pee-Bee?' Toni frowned. 'Who's that?'

'Philip Benjamin Lambert – Benny,' John explained. 'We've had a few run-ins with him, mainly when he's got into fights. They used to call him Pee-Bee when he was at school and some of his old chums would wind him up when they were in the pub by calling him that. He's not a bad lad, just a bit volatile and, well, not the sharpest tack in the box.'

'Is he capable of murder?' Toni asked.

'Anyone is capable of murder,' Agatha said, 'but not everyone is wicked enough to plan a murder in advance.'

'Benny wouldn't plan to go out and kill someone,' John said. 'Any time he's got into trouble, it's been down to someone teasing him either about the name or about Elizabeth. He won't hear a word said against her.'

'Hmm . . .' Agatha mused. 'I'm inclined to think that Gerald and Petula are still our prime suspects. Perhaps Stephanie can help us make some headway there . . . In the meantime, let's take some tea down to the Parsonses – they must be parched with all that dancing!'

Chapter Eight

Agatha was woken the following morning not by her usual radio alarm, but by the chirping of her phone. When she checked the time, it was barely 4 a.m. There was no caller identity on her screen. She hit the button to take the call.

'Who is this?' she said. 'If you're phoning from a call centre in Delhi to try to sell me life insurance or broadband, I'm getting on the next flight to India and I'm going to—'

'Mrs Raisin! It's me!' came a vaguely familiar voice.

'Who's . . . wait . . . Spider? Why the hell are you calling me at this hour?'

'You told me to! It's a boy! It's a beautiful baby boy! Never seen nothin' like it in my whole life! Beautiful – just like his mum!'

'That's . . . very nice, Spider,' Agatha said, stifling a yawn. 'Are Amy and the baby both okay?'

'Both perfect! You should come see him, Mrs Raisin! He's the best thing ever!'

'I will . . . I will . . . maybe once you've had a chance to get some sleep.'

'I can't sleep! I have to tell everyone. This is just . . . the most brilliant thing ever. I'm makin' plans. I need to get a job. I need to get Amy and the baby out of that scuzzy flat, get him nice clothes and . . . suchlike. Everything's going to change now, Mrs Raisin. I'm gonna change – you'll see.'

'I'm sure you will, Spider. Er . . . do you have a name for the baby?'

'Grayson. Grayson Hendricks.'

'That's . . . a nice name. Unusual. What made you think of it?'

'Heard it at the Archers. Some used to call the targets Graysons. I kind of liked the name.'

Spider then babbled about having other people to phone and rang off. Agatha stared at her phone screen, marvelling at the transformation that seemed to have overcome Spider. Was it real? Would it last? Not my problem, she decided, but I might as well have a shower now. I'm wide awake. Then her phone screen light went out, leaving her in darkness. No I'm not, she thought, curled up and went back to sleep.

A little over three hours later, Agatha was showered, dressed and sipping her first coffee of the day, planning her tactics and ready to do battle. Her main adversary that morning, she decided, was Gerald Pride, and she was to attack what she felt was his weak spot – his wife, Stephanie. Divide and conquer – that's the way forward, she told herself, dumping her coffee cup in the kitchen sink and grabbing her car keys. Some might think Stephanie Pride, with her blonde hair and her nasty temper, was a force to be reckoned with, but she hadn't yet crossed swords with Agatha Raisin!

Within half an hour, Agatha was sitting in her car in one of Lower Burlip's most exclusive avenues, looking across the road at the house where Gerald and Stephanie Pride lived. It was clearly an affluent area, a wide, tree-lined boulevard with large front gardens and driveways big enough to accommodate several cars. The houses looked like they had all been built in the 1920s or 1930s, each one individually architect-designed, each one different from its neighbour, but all of Cotswold stone beneath slate roofs with large bay windows and solid wooden front doors. They were the sort of houses where she imagined the original owners to have been wealthy local businesspeople, bank managers or surgeons.

She waited, and watched, until Gerald Pride appeared, carrying his briefcase. He got into his car, reversed out of the driveway and headed off towards town. She waited a while longer to be certain that he wouldn't suddenly reappear, having forgotten his phone or a document or his wallet. He didn't. She left her car parked in the street and walked purposefully up the drive to ring the doorbell. A few moments later, Stephanie Pride opened the door. Her blonde mane looked a little unkempt and she was without make-up, wearing only a long and, Agatha judged, very expensive silk dressing gown. At first, she seemed a little surprised to see Agatha standing there, and then simply amused.

'You again,' she said. 'What do you want?'

'I think we should talk,' Agatha replied in a matter-of-fact tone, 'about Carseworth Manor ... and your husband.'

'Why would I want to talk to you about anything?'

'Because we're each in a position to get the other exactly what she wants.'

'You think you know what I want?' Stephanie laughed. 'I'm intrigued, Mrs Raisin. You'd best come in.'

She led the way into the house through a reception hall that boasted wood panelling to waist level. To Agatha, the place looked very much like a family home deluding itself that it was a grand house – a less elaborate, smaller attempt to impersonate Carseworth Manor. Agatha followed Stephanie through to a modern kitchen looking out over a well-tended large garden laid to lawn surrounded by flower beds and enclosed by tall hedges. She took a seat at the kitchen table while Stephanie made coffee.

'Can I tempt you with something stronger?' Stephanie asked, waggling a bottle of brandy. 'I've often seen people in cafés in Europe – from Belgium to Italy – having a small brandy, a glass of wine or a beer with their morning coffee before they go to work. It sets you up for the day.'

'Not for me, thanks,' Agatha said, watching Stephanie slosh some brandy into a tumbler. 'You enjoy travelling, then?'

'Don't you? There are so many wonderful places to visit in Europe, and it's practically on our doorstep. Takes no time at all to fly south, but you land in a different world. So much more sophisticated, so much more glamorous than boring old Mircester.'

'You're right,' Agatha agreed, accepting a stylish coffee cup and saucer. 'There are so many things to see and experience out there. I've travelled quite a bit in Europe and around the Med. I've often thought how much better it would be to live there rather than here.' She could see she had caught Stephanie's interest, quickly concluding that her best tactic was to entice her with the promise of an easy way to fabulous wealth. 'Of course, you need to have money to do it in style.'

'And that's how you can get me what I want, is it? You can get me the kind of money I'd need for that? How do you propose to do that?'

'We need to talk about your husband first. How are things between you two?'

'Ha! You obviously know that ours is not what most people would call a perfect marriage.'

'People have very different ideas about how a marriage should work. Some can be very understanding, quite tolerant, of their partner's . . . transgressions.'

'You're talking about Gerald being unfaithful?' Stephanie made a theatrical pretence at being shocked. 'Oh, how could he?' Then she laughed. 'You think I don't know about him and that little scrubber Petula?'

'In my experience, the wife almost always knows. Knowing what to do about it is a different matter.'

'How can you help me with that? I'm not about to divorce him unless I can get a major pay-out, and at the

172

moment all I stand to get is half of this house – which is mine by rights anyway!'

'I can get the deal to sell Carseworth Manor back on track.'

Stephanie leaned forward on the table, suddenly serious. Agatha looked her straight in the eye.

'An associate of mine was negotiating the spa deal with Sir Godfrey on behalf of a London businessman. My associate is no longer involved and I've taken over.'

'But Gerald will never go for that deal.'

'It's worth a lot more than anything else he could come up with. All we have to do is make him, as the saying goes, "an offer he can't refuse".'

'He's stubborn. He'll just say no.'

'Not if the alternative is going to jail and losing the lot.'

'What are you talking about? Why would he go to jail?'

'For the murder of his father.'

'Are you serious? You could never make that stick. I know for a fact that he was here when the old boy was killed. We left the fete together and came straight back here.'

'I know. I saw you go, but you mustn't underestimate what I can achieve in a very short space of time, Mrs Pride. In my business, I get to know a lot of people. I do them favours and they do me favours. I have a couple of police friends who owe me big time. The police are still running tests on the body of the old man and the arrow used to kill him. All I need is a couple of hairs from your husband's brush or comb to snag in the fletches – the feathered flight things on the arrow – and I can get someone to plant them there. DNA tests will show him to be the murderer.'

'But he's already told the police he was here with me when it happened, and I confirmed that.'

'So you tell the police that he forced you to say that. This is a big house. Tell them that you didn't have sight of him the whole time, so you can't be sure he didn't sneak off back to the fete. That blows his alibi out of the water.'

'He couldn't have left here without me knowing, but even if I lie about that, how does any of it get us the property deal?'

'The police will question him when the hairs are discovered. He knows he didn't kill his father, so he'll know that the evidence must have been planted. I'll tell him I can make it disappear as easily as I put it there – but only if he signs the deal.'

'You can do that?'

'It's really not as difficult as you might think.'

Stephanie swirled the brandy in her glass, took a sip and thought for a moment.

'I've got a better idea,' she said eventually. 'Get him to agree to the deal but don't make the evidence disappear. We'll send the bastard to jail anyway!'

'I like the way you think.' Agatha nodded, smiling.

'Come with me,' Stephanie said, jumping to her feet. 'We'll get you what you need.'

Ten minutes later, Agatha was back sitting in her car. She let out a huge sigh of relief, leaning her head against the steering wheel. Then she took her phone from her handbag and hit a speed-dial number.

'John?' she said when he answered. 'Yes, it's me . . . Yes, I'm sure I sound a bit funny. That's probably because I've just told the biggest pack of lies in my entire life, but it's got us one step forward on the murder case and I think I've worked out how we can nail Freddy Evans . . . but I need your help.'

By the time she reached her office, the staff of Raisin Investigations were all at their desks, as Agatha expected. They all looked up as she walked in.

'Heard you had a good result on the Parsons case, boss,' Simon said, cheerily.

'A straightforward tail,' Agatha said with a complacent smile, 'and, in the end, a straightforward tale.'

'I saw what you did there, boss.' Simon laughed. 'Good wordsmithing!'

'Wordsmithing? Is that even a thing?' She frowned at him, then turned to Patrick. 'How are your preparations for the big match this evening?'

'All going smoothly,' Patrick reported. 'We'll get over there later this morning to make sure everything's ready. That'll give us a chance to have another root around.'

'Good.' Agatha turned to Toni. 'It was a boy. Mother and child doing well. They're calling him Grayson.'

'Unusual name,' Toni said, nodding her approval. 'Sounds cool.'

'Should we . . . send something?' Agatha asked.

'Flowers for Amy, a baby-grow or something for Grayson, and a card,' Toni advised.

'Would you sort that out, Toni? I know they're still suspects but it could be useful to be on friendly terms with them.'

Helen appeared by Agatha's side with her mail and a cup of coffee.

'Thank you, Helen. I'll be in my office but I don't want to be disturbed. I have some plotting and scheming to do.'

Agatha sat at her desk, sipping her coffee. She pushed the mail aside, placed her phone in front of her and stared at it. She ran through dozens of conversations in her head, or rather snatches of conversations – what she would say, what might be said to her, how she might respond. She might only get one crack at this and she had to do it right. If she slipped up and aroused suspicion, it was all over. She gulped down some coffee, picked up the phone and dialled a number given to her by Roy. The phone was answered straight away.

'Good morning, Mr Evans, my name is Agatha Raisin.' Agatha spoke clearly in a pleasant, businesslike manner. 'I'm an associate of Roy Silver.'

'Yeah, I know who you are,' Freddy Evans replied bluntly. 'What do you want?'

'You probably don't know that Mr Silver is currently in hospital. The police think that he was the victim of some sort of mugging gone wrong.'

'Is that so? Shame. Nothin' to do with me, though.'

'Nothing to do with . . .' Agatha took a deep breath to help keep her temper under control, and carried on. 'No, of course not, Mr Evans, although I do know that Mr

Silver was helping you put a deal together for the purchase of Carseworth Manor.'

'You seem to know a lot about my business, Mrs Raisin.'

'Just this one deal, really, Mr Evans. You see, I was able to introduce Roy to Gerald Pride, Sir Godfrey Pride's son, and while Mr Pride was originally reluctant to enter into negotiations for the sale of Carseworth, he's now been in touch to let me know that he may be willing to reconsider.'

'Has he really, now? And why would you be takin' an interest in this?'

'Let's be frank, Mr Evans.' Agatha let out a heavy sigh, mainly for effect. 'I'm a businesswoman and I'm not doing this out of the goodness of my heart. Silver's now out of the picture. I can get you the deal but I want his fee plus the PR contract for the new spa and leisure operation.'

'You'd sell your old pal Silver down the river, just like that?'

'Business is business, Mr Evans. Silver couldn't hack it, but I can. He used to work for me, you know. The big difference is that now you're dealing with the organ grinder, not the monkey.'

'We need to talk – but not on the phone.'

'I know a quiet pub where we can meet – the Red Lion in Carsely. Would seven o'clock tomorrow evening suit you? I can get us a table where we won't be disturbed.'

'Carsely? I'll find it. See you there.'

He hung up. Agatha stared at her phone, drumming the fingers of her free hand on the table. Evans had taken the bait . . . or had he? He was a shrewd operator and she couldn't afford the slightest mistake if she was to reel him in. Worse still, if it all went wrong, she could end up in Mircester General just like Roy.

Agatha worked until disturbing rumblings from her stomach told her that lunchtime was fast approaching. Patrick and Simon had gone when she walked out into the main office but she was able to entice Toni across the cobbled lane outside with the promise of a pub lunch at the King Charles. Agatha brought Toni up to speed with her Stephanie Pride encounter.

'So she really believes you're going to frame her husband?' Toni said, trailing her fork through her tuna salad.

'I'm pretty sure she does,' Agatha nodded, tucking into sausages and mash with gravy. 'I can't see why she would play along otherwise. In any case, I got what I needed from it. Now, about Freddy Evans . . .'

Once Toni was fully briefed, and they had each enjoyed a small glass of wine, Agatha announced that she was taking the rest of the day off.

'James is coming home at some point,' she explained, 'but they're not sure when they'll be ready to let him out, so he's insisted on taking a taxi rather than me picking him up. I want to be there for him when he gets back, though. I don't want him coming home to an empty house.'

'You're not going to cook for him, are you?'

'What's that supposed to mean?'

'Well, he's only just got out of hospital. You don't want to send him straight back in again.'

'Are you saying that my cooking is . . .' Agatha watched Toni's face break into a smile, then her shoulders shake with a suppressed chuckle, and knew she'd been had. She was not pleased. She looked at her watch and tapped it with her forefinger. 'Time you were back at work, isn't it?' she said, then gathered her coat and handbag and left.

Agatha sat in her living room, engrossed in the *Mircester Telegraph*, reading one of Charlotte Clark's reports on how the police were no further forward with their investigation into the Pride murder, with a quote from DCI Wilkes attempting to contradict her by saying that he 'expected to make an arrest in due course'. Does he think that's going to be me, she wondered? She gave a derisive snort. The man was an imbecile. It was then that she looked out her front window to see James stepping out of a taxi.

Rushing to her front door, she skipped over the low fence that divided their properties and met James on his garden path. He was wearing a dark blue blazer and grey flannels, his shoes were polished and his shirt was freshly laundered. He looked every inch the former military man, but his tall frame, normally straight as a parade-ground flagpole, was slightly stooped, making him appear a little weary. Behind him, he dragged a small suitcase on wheels.

'Welcome home!' she said, taking the handle of his case, and looking down at the walking stick in his other hand. 'Are you feeling a bit unsteady?'

'This thing?' he said, tucking it under his arm like a swagger stick. 'Not really necessary. I'm pretty much right as rain.'

'Let's get you inside,' she said. 'I'll make you some tea.'

'Sun's past the yard arm,' he replied, grinning. 'How about a gin-and-tonic instead?'

'Sounds perfect!'

James sat in a leather armchair in his living room while Agatha raided his drinks cabinet. Unlike her own living room, which was cosy and characterful, a perfect place to relax, Agatha had always found James's a bit too formal. The two chairs were arranged at precisely the same angle to the sofa, the framed photographs on the walls were all perfectly aligned and even in the drinks cabinet, the bottles stood to attention like guardsmen on parade.

She fetched some ice from the kitchen, handed James his drink and they clinked glasses.

'It's very nice to be back,' he said, 'and there's no one in the world I'd rather come home to.'

'I was thinking that the other day,' she said. 'Life simply wouldn't be the same if I didn't have you next door.'

'So, shall we plan our great escape to somewhere warm and sunny?'

'Let's get you settled in first. I don't think you're quite ready to go jetting off anywhere just yet.'

'I thought we might pop open a laptop and browse a few destinations on the internet.'

'Maybe not today, James. We've plenty time for that later.'

'You don't want to come with me, do you?'

'It's not that ... I'm just, well, a bit busy at the moment ... I can't think about going away right now. Let's leave it a few days.'

'I see,' he said, staring down at his drink before taking a swig, standing and placing it on the mantelpiece. 'Well, I have a case to unpack and some mail to sort through, so ...'

There could be no doubt about it. James had just invited her to leave. Even though Agatha gave him a hug and kissed his cheek, there was no ignoring the fact that the atmosphere between them, if not entirely frosty, had turned distinctly chilly. She stepped over the fence between their front gardens and opened her own front door to find a slip of paper lying on the mat. She unfolded it and read the stark message.

IF YOU WANT TO KNOW WHO KILLED SIR GODFREY, MEET ME AT THE GRAVE OF GRAYSON PRIDE AT ELEVEN TONIGHT.
COME ALONE.
A

Refolding the note, she walked through to the kitchen, puzzling over its contents. There was that name again – Grayson. Was it a Pride family name? Where was the grave? Could it be in St Jude's churchyard? She put in a call to Margaret Bloxby.

'Hello, Agatha,' Mrs Bloxby answered after a few rings. 'How are you?'

'I'm fine, thanks,' Agatha said, resisting the temptation to embark on a lengthy discourse about all that had been happening, 'but I have a question to which you may well know the answer.'

'Fire away.'

'Have you ever heard of Grayson Pride?'

'Yes, I think he's one of the Prides residing in our graveyard.'

'Can you show me where?'

'Of course. Why don't you pop round in about half an hour?'

Agatha gratefully agreed to pay Mrs Bloxby a visit, then phoned Sir Charles Fraith. Her call was answered after three rings by Gustav's unmistakable, overripe baritone.

'Barfield House.'

'Gustav, it's me. I need to talk to Charles.'

'Sir Charles is rather busy at the moment, Mrs Raisin. I suggest you try . . .'

'Gustav!' Agatha could hear Charles yelling from his desk in the library to where she knew Gustav was standing at the telephone table in the hall. 'Stop messing about and put her through!'

There was a tut and a sigh from Gustav, then a click from the phone before Charles came on the line.

'Aggieeee . . . atha,' Charles corrected himself before Agatha could scold him. 'Why do you always phone on the landline? You can get straight through to me on my mobile.'

'Charles, you know full well that's not true. You can never find your mobile. It's always down the back of a sofa or in the pocket of a jacket you haven't worn for a week.'

'True. You know me so well. How goes it with the murder?'

'I'm now making some progress,' she said. 'I wanted to ask you about the Pride family. Do you still have a copy of that old manuscript?'

'I do. Funnily enough, after our chat the other day, I looked it out. It's sitting right here on my desk.'

'I'm interested in Grayson Pride. Is there any mention of him?'

'I should think so. There's a family tree at the beginning of this thing . . .' Agatha could hear Charles shuffling papers. 'Yes, there he is, in the seventeenth century . . . in the manuscript, that should put him around here . . . what do you need to know?'

'I'm not sure. Anything unusual about him?'

'Well, if we can believe what's in here, he met a bit of a sticky end. He was shot with an arrow by his pregnant lover!'

'Was he indeed?' Agatha said slowly. 'Thanks for that, Charles. Must dash, I have a grave to visit!'

Mrs Bloxby spotted Agatha walking along the street towards the church and met her by the rectory gate.

'Why the sudden interest in old graves?' she asked.

'You know I'm looking into the murder of Sir Godfrey?' Agatha said.

'Everyone does. There's not a soul in Carsely who would think, even for a moment, that Agatha Raisin could come across a body and not launch her own investigation.'

'Well, this is sort of background stuff.' Agatha hated lying to Mrs Bloxby but, for the time being, she had to keep the existence of the note and the meeting that night a secret. 'It can't hurt to know more about the Pride family.'

Mrs Bloxby led Agatha into the graveyard and over to a corner where the ancient headstones were the most eroded she had ever seen, crumbling like flaking pastry. Some graves were marked with flat stone slabs and any words inscribed on those were so weathered as to be illegible.

'I think I remember seeing Grayson's name around here,' Mrs Bloxby said, examining a clutch of headstones close to the trees at the edge of the graveyard. 'It's always surprised me that the Prides never erected some kind of mausoleum or family tomb but they seemed content to be laid to rest in the open, apart from a couple who are under ledger stones in the floor of the church. Ah . . . here he is.'

Mrs Bloxby pointed to a grave where part of the name 'Grayson' was visible, but little else.

'It's in pretty poor condition,' Agatha noted.

'It's been standing out here in all weathers for nearly four centuries without the benefit of all those expensive face creams you use!' Mrs Bloxby laughed. 'So it's showing its age far more than you ever will.'

'Yes, it's too far gone even for Botox or a little tuck here and there,' Agatha agreed, smiling. 'Not that I've ever had . . .'

'No, of course not – perish the thought.'

They walked back out into the street together and no sooner had they turned towards the rectory than a scruffy Land Rover screeched to a halt beside them. Benny Lambert was at the wheel. Elizabeth Pride leaned out the passenger window.

'My brother tells me you've been prying into our family affairs, Mrs Raisin,' she said, her face a mask of grim menace.

'Affairs – that's an interesting word to choose.' Agatha returned her stare, unblinking. 'You and Gerald are back on speaking terms, then?'

'That's none of your concern. I talk to my brother when I need to and nothing that we say or do, absolutely nothing about the Pride family, is any of your business.'

'I found your father in the woods,' Agatha pointed out. 'I heard his final words. I watched the poor man take his last breath. I held his hand as he died. I think that makes Sir Godfrey Pride my business.'

'I'm warning you – just stay away from us, or you'll regret it!' Elizabeth snarled, then muttered to Benny and the Land Rover shot off in the direction of Carseworth Manor.

'She's always been somewhat headstrong,' said Mrs Bloxby.

'Headstrong or not,' Agatha said, watching the car disappear into the distance, 'Elizabeth Pride made a big mistake threatening me!'

'Don't go doing anything rash.'

'Would I ever?'

'Actually, yes, Mrs Raisin,' Mrs Bloxby said, standing with her hands on her hips and reverting to the Carsely Ladies Society formal form of address, the grin on her face showing she was having fun. 'Rash moves are practically your modus operandi.'

'In that case, Mrs Bloxby,' Agatha said, laughing, 'I will do my best to stay out of trouble.'

'Good. Now – how about a small sherry back at the rectory?'

'I'd love to . . . but some other time, if that's all right. I have a lot to do tonight and I need to keep a clear head.'

Agatha stared at herself in her full-length bedroom mirror. She was wearing black walking shoes, black trousers, a black sweater and a black jacket. Too casual for a funeral, she thought, although there had been plenty where she was going. Should she be going at all, though? A meeting in a graveyard under cover of darkness was melodramatic enough almost to be comic, but there was always the chance she was walking into danger. The note, like the one that had apparently lured Sir Godfrey into the woods, could so easily be tempting her into a trap. But what if it wasn't? What if the mysterious 'A' could hand her the murderer on a plate? That, of course, was the bait in the trap.

She straightened her jacket and nodded to herself. She could deal with it. She'd scouted the graveyard that afternoon with Margaret Bloxby. She would take cover in the trees until she could see who was coming to meet her, then she would handle the situation as she saw fit. Nobody was going to catch her unawares.

Agatha left her cottage via the back door, flitting through the shadows in her garden to the very end, where she pushed her way through a gap in the hedge and swung herself over the high fence onto a narrow path. She waited, trying to control her breathing, watching and listening. There was just enough daylight left to make out the bushes and trees that bordered the fields at the back of her house. She had chosen this route in order to avoid anyone who might be watching for her leaving in the more conventional manner along Lilac Lane to the high street. There was no point hiding in the woods if someone simply followed her in there.

With no hint of anyone in the vicinity, she made her way to the field and trotted along its perimeter, crouched low, sticking to the shadows. She would be early for the graveyard rendezvous, having left plenty of time to conceal herself in the trees. It would be dark soon, heavy clouds hiding the bright harvest moon that would otherwise have lit up the countryside like a celestial searchlight. Crossing a ditch into the field where the fete had been held, she crept through the gathering gloom in the woods until she reached a spot near the edge of the graveyard, close to Grayson Pride's headstone.

She knelt at the base of a tree, peering into the graveyard. It was already too dark to make out any details, the gravestones reduced to indistinct mounds, the trees and the church spire towering black shapes. Beyond the graveyard, streetlights twinkled through the trees, but their illumination failed to penetrate the darkness this far away. She settled down, checking that her phone was in silent mode. The last thing she wanted was her ringtone blasting out and giving her away. She also checked the slim pen-torch in her pocket, shielding the light with her hand. Now all she had to do was wait.

Agatha didn't have to wait long. As soon as the darkness had closed in completely, but long before the appointed hour, she heard the rustle of leaves somewhere at the edge of the trees. Those were footsteps, she was sure of it. Someone was attempting to do what she had done and find a vantage point prior to the meeting. No, not someone. There were two people. She could hear two sets of footsteps and even, when she strained hard, a muffled whisper and a hushed voice in response. She had come alone, but whoever else was visiting the graveyard had not! She waited until they drew closer, then decided to act.

'That's far enough!' she called, stepping out from behind her tree. 'Stay right where you are!'

She clicked on her torch, aiming it in the direction of the footsteps, and briefly picked out two figures before they ducked into cover behind a tree. The next thing she knew, she was caught in the dazzlingly bright white beam of an extremely powerful flashlight. There was a juddering thud beside her head and, to her horror, she saw an arrow embedded in the tree trunk. Someone was trying to shoot her!

'Snakes and bastards!' she hissed, dropping her torch, flinging herself to the ground and rolling away from the tree into cover behind one of the larger gravestones. The powerful light beam went out and there was darkness once more. She blinked hard, for a few moments seeing only spots and swirls. Her eyes had become accustomed to the dark and the light had destroyed her night vision.

She reached for her phone, then suddenly wondered why they had switched off their light. So that I can't see where they are, she decided – but they saw me diving in here. They must be moving round to get another clear shot. She had to move! Leaping to her feet, she sprinted into the dark, then yelped as her knee smacked into a gravestone. She stumbled and her phone flew out of her hand. She heard it shatter against a stone somewhere in front of her. The headstone she had run into then toppled over, smashing itself on what Agatha assumed was a slab with an almighty crack that echoed into the night.

The flashlight suddenly lit up the graveyard again and Agatha dived behind another headstone too quickly for the archer to take aim and loose an arrow. The light was quickly extinguished. She looked towards the streetlights. That's where she had to go. She had to get to the street, or the rectory. She would be safe there – or was she safer where she was? Curled up behind the headstone, she wanted to melt into its crumbling face, disappear so that dreadful light could never find her. It was easier to stay where she was. Her legs were trembling, her hands shaking and she could hear her breath coming in short sobs. She couldn't move. No – she had to move. She had to move now, otherwise the next time that light came on she'd be as dead as whoever was lying in the grave she was squatting on!

She forced herself to her feet and ran, only to see the beam of a weak torch bobbing in the dark in front of her.

'Who's out there?' came Mrs Bloxby's voice. 'What's going on? I've called the police!'

'Margaret!' Agatha screamed. 'Get back!'

At that moment, there was a flood of light once more and Agatha gasped as she felt, and heard, an arrow swishing past her ear. Then she saw Margaret Bloxby, also caught in the light, stagger forward and sink to the ground, the arrow lodged in her chest.

'No! No!' Agatha screamed, running towards her friend. 'Margaret!'

The light went out, but Agatha could see Mrs Bloxby's fallen shape on the ground, highlighted by the yellow beam of her own torch. She was lying on her back, the arrow standing straight and proud, with a spreading stain of blood seeping across the front of her T-shirt. Agatha held Margaret's hand and stroked her forehead.

'Margaret!' she shouted. 'Stay with me! Open your eyes, Margaret!'

There was no response.

'Help!' Agatha howled. 'Somebody help us! Please – help!'

She looked round but could see no sign of anyone. Above the trees she could make out the dark silhouette of the church spire, and Agatha Raisin, who had never had much time for religion, now resorted to seeking help from above.

'Margaret Bloxby's God!' she howled, tears streaming down her face. 'If you're out there, you better do something about this right now, you hear me? You can't let this woman go! She's one of yours! She's the best you ever made! You can't let her die! You have to save her! She can't die . . . please . . . she's my friend . . .'

Chapter Nine

'Worst . . . prayer ever,' came a whispered voice.

Agatha looked down at Margaret to see her eyes flickering open.

'Margaret!' she gasped. 'You're alive! Don't try to talk. I'll . . . I'll get help.'

'Phone,' Margaret breathed, with a huge effort.

'I can't,' Agatha groaned. 'My phone was smashed to pieces.'

'My . . . phone.' Margaret raised her left hand to show her mobile phone, lifting the small device clearly requiring so much effort that it seemed to weigh as much as one of the gravestones that surrounded them in the darkness.

'Brilliant!' Agatha cried. 'And didn't you say you already called the police?'

'I . . . lied.'

'You lied? Bugger!' Agatha took the phone and stared at the keypad. The quickest way to get help would be to call John, or maybe Bill. They knew how to get the emergency services here fastest – but who remembers phone numbers nowadays? They're stored in your phone's memory so that you didn't have to keep them in your own memory. 'Bugger!' she repeated.

'Less swearing . . . more dialling,' Margaret said.

Agatha punched a number into the keypad and got it right first time when John answered.

'John!' she yelled. 'It's me! Margaret's been shot with an arrow! We're in St Jude's churchyard. She's bleeding – we need help!'

'Stay right where you are,' John advised. 'Keep her conscious. Don't try to move her. I'll call you right back.'

He rang off. The silence made it feel like the darkness was closing in around the feeble glow of Margaret's torch. Agatha shouted at Margaret that help was on its way.

'I know,' she replied, grimacing in pain. 'Being shot . . . with an arrow . . . doesn't make you deaf.'

At that moment the phone rang.

'Agatha, stay on the line,' John said. 'Put me on speaker so Margaret can hear. We both need to talk to her to keep her conscious.'

Agatha did as instructed and John kept talking.

'An ambulance is on its way, Margaret,' he said. 'It will be there in minutes. Agatha, be prepared to shout, jump around, flash a light, anything to guide them to you. I'll be with you in no time at all. Did you see who did this? Are they still around?'

The thought that the two stalkers might still be out there suddenly hit home and Agatha slowly scanned the darkness, picking out the shadowy shapes of bushes and headstones, straining to spot any sign of movement. There was none.

'They've gone,' she said. 'They must have run off. They've had plenty of time. If they were still here, they'd have finished what they came to do.'

Moments later, she could hear sirens, and before she knew it the graveyard was bright with lights, swarming with paramedics and police officers, and John was by her side.

'John!' she sobbed, flinging her arms around his shoulders and burying her face in his chest. 'It's so awful. They were trying to get me and they got Margaret!'

'It's okay,' he said, softly. 'We can go into all that later.'

He was looking over at where the paramedics were working on Margaret. One of them, whom Agatha recognised as Denise, the same woman who had tended to Roy, stood and walked towards them. She nodded a greeting to Agatha.

'It's a really nasty wound,' she explained. 'Had it been just a couple of inches lower to the left, she wouldn't have stood a chance. We won't know for sure how bad it really is until we take her in, but the arrow has missed the vital organs. She's stable and breathing well and there's not too much blood loss. The big danger now is infection and . . .'

'What's going on here? Where is my wife?' The voice of the Reverend Bloxby cut through the crackle and bleep of personal radios and the confusion of a dozen conversations. 'Margaret?' he called, spotting the figure on the ground, and then, as it dawned on him that it really was her lying there, 'Margaret!'

He rushed forward only for John to envelop him in a massive bear hug.

'Easy now,' he said. 'She's in good hands. You have to let them do their job. Give her all the support you can, but don't interfere.'

When Alf Bloxby's legs started to give way, John gently lowered the vicar to the ground and he scrambled over to where his wife lay. Taking her hand, he spoke soothingly to her and Margaret shifted her head a fraction to look at him, closing her fingers around his.

Agatha explained to John how she had come to be in the graveyard that night and how her attackers had stalked her. He spoke with a number of uniformed officers and Agatha watched them seal off the area. Beyond the portable lights now illuminating the immediate area, she could see torch beams flickering in the woods where officers were checking to ensure that Agatha's pursuers were not lurking in the darkness, hiding until the coast was clear.

'I can't believe you came here alone,' he said, a note of harsh rebuke in his tone. 'You should have called me. This was obviously a trap. You put yourself in terrible danger.'

'Maybe,' Agatha shrugged, 'but that was my choice. I thought I could handle it. Now Margaret's the one who's suffering.'

'Those paramedics are the best in the business. They'll take care of her, Agatha. She's going to be okay – I know she is – but you mustn't blame yourself for what happened.'

When the medics were ready to move Margaret, four lifted the stretcher, taking a corner each, keeping their patient absolutely level and stable. Another walked alongside, holding up an intravenous drip. They picked their way, slowly and delicately, through the graveyard to the ambulance. Alf stayed as close as he could to the stretcher and Agatha followed immediately behind, accompanied by John. Margaret was then carefully loaded into the ambulance, an oxygen mask covering her face and the arrow still sticking grotesquely up from her body.

'I should go with her,' Agatha said, moving forward, but her way was immediately barred by Alf.

'You'll do no such thing!' he barked, glaring at her with undiluted fury. 'I will go with my wife and you will stay well away. I don't want to see you anywhere near Margaret. You are nothing but trouble, Agatha Raisin! I was only gone for two hours and came back to all this – my wife, shot! Look at her – she's in agony! And this is all your fault!'

He climbed into the back of the ambulance, Agatha taking a step back, stunned by Alf's vehemence. Just before the doors were slammed shut, she saw a slight movement of Margaret's left hand. It formed an unmistakable 'thumbs up', pointed directly at her. Margaret wanted her to know they were still friends, despite what her husband had said.

'The vicar didn't mean that,' John said, putting his arm around her. 'He's just upset. Who wouldn't be? We all are, but it's not your fault.'

'Yes, it is,' Agatha said, biting her lip. 'If I hadn't come here tonight, this would never have happened.'

'But you didn't kill Sir Godfrey. You didn't write those notes. You didn't come here to commit murder – and you didn't fire that arrow. This is *not* your fault.'

'It should have been me, John. The arrow was meant for me. I wish they'd got me. Rather me than Margaret. She did nothing to deserve this.'

'Neither did you, although this does beg the question – why? Why lure you into a trap? Why try to kill you? You've got somebody very worried. Clearly whoever murdered Sir Godfrey thinks you're getting too close.'

'That could be any two of a number of . . . Oh, I can't think about that right now.' She watched the ambulance depart while John took a phone call. 'All I can think about is poor Margaret.'

'I'm afraid we need to go into town, Agatha,' John said. 'Wilkes is on his way into the station and he wants to interview you.'

'Wilkes – really? That's all I need.'

'We'd have been taking a statement from you anyway,' John said with a shrug, 'and Wilkes would then have wanted to talk to you in any case. I guess this kills two birds with one stone.'

'Right,' Agatha said, gritting her teeth and marching towards the street. 'Let's get it over with.'

Sitting in the interview room where John had left her with a cup of tea and the promise that he would be back shortly reminded Agatha of sitting in the hospital corridor. It was a room in an institution, undecorated and unloved. It wasn't the sort of room she'd seen on TV cop shows with a huge mirror, behind which the interrogators lurked in the darkness, observing the suspect without being seen themselves. In fact, it was a bare, sad little room furnished with just a table and four chairs. It was clean in the same way that the hospital was clean – clean but not comfortable. Unlike the hospital, at least it didn't smell of disinfectant and overused toilets.

The door opened and Wilkes walked in, a document folder under his arm and a copy of the statement Agatha had given to John in his other hand. John was at his shoulder and gave her a meaningful look, the meaning being, 'Just behave!'

'Ah, Mrs Raisin!' Wilkes gave her a slimy smile. 'I'd like to say what a pleasure it is to see you again . . . but it's not.'

'I bet you've been practising that line all day!' Agatha laughed, without any humour. 'It's sad that you've had three days to come up with something clever to say, and that's the best you could do. You're pathetic, Wilkes.'

Wilkes pursed his lips, slapped the folder down on the table and sat opposite her. John took the adjacent chair, staying slightly further away from the table, out of Wilkes's eye line.

'You are honoured, Mrs Raisin, to be interviewed by two such senior officers,' Wilkes said pompously. 'Normally we'd leave the likes of you to a constable, but DI Glass insisted on being present and there are several things that I would like to hear you explain to me.'

'Several things?' Agatha sounded concerned. 'That sounds like a lot for you to take in, but I'll do my best.

Would you like some time to go warm up your brain cell?'

'Oh, very funny, Mrs Raisin, but I didn't come here to . . .' Wilkes looked round at John, who was drawing a finger aggressively across his throat, trying to get Agatha to back off. 'Are you all right, Glass?'

'Ahh . . . yes, sir,' John said, quickly tugging at his collar. 'This collar's just irritating my neck a bit.'

Wilkes eyed him suspiciously, then turned back to Agatha.

'Your statement,' he said, waving the document at her, 'is very disturbing. It throws up a number of questions but, most of all, it clearly shows that you are interfering in a police investigation. I'm inclined to arrest you right now and charge you under the 1996 Police Act for obstructing an officer . . .'

John tapped the table to attract Wilkes's attention, then wrinkled his nose and gave a little shake of his head. Wilkes stared at him.

'No . . .? Then perhaps we can make it wasting police time,' Wilkes said, changing tack. 'Under the 1967 Criminal Law Act, you could get six months for that!'

John sighed and shook his head again.

'If you are stupid enough to arrest me without due cause and cast-iron evidence,' Agatha wagged a warning finger at Wilkes, 'I will sue Mircester Police for wrongful arrest and you, personally, for the distress caused by your persistent persecution of me! By the time I'm finished with you, you'll be out of a job and you can kiss your pension goodbye!'

Wilkes leaned back in his chair for a discreet word with John.

'Can she do that?'

John gave a resigned nod.

'You know, Glass,' Wilkes said, turning to face John properly, 'sometimes I wonder just whose side you're on!'

'It's not a question of sides,' John said. 'Doing the right thing is what matters.'

'Doing what I tell you is all that should matter to you, Inspector!' Wilkes snarled.

'It's *you* who should be charged with wasting police time!' John's temper was beginning to get the better of him. Agatha frantically drew a finger back and forwards across her throat but his focus was entirely on Wilkes. 'You should be concentrating on pursuing the investigation in the proper manner instead of using it to try to get at Agatha!'

'Oh . . . it's "Agatha" now, is it?' Wilkes gave a sly, knowing smile. 'I see. She's got you wrapped around her little finger, hasn't she, Glass? Used her womanly wiles to lure you into the bedroom, did she? I bet you'd do whatever she wanted once she'd got you between the sheets! That's the way tarts like her get their own way!'

John gave a roar and launched himself at Wilkes, grabbing him round the throat. Agatha was on the other side of the table in the blink of an eye, inserting herself between them.

'Now, now, boys,' she scolded them, using the voice

she normally reserved for Boswell and Hodge. 'I, for one, have had quite enough of this, so I'm declaring the inter-view over.'

'You haven't heard the last of this, Glass!' Wilkes hissed, grabbing his document folder and storming out of the room.

'Thanks,' John said, breathing heavily. 'If you hadn't stepped in, I'd have . . .'

'I know,' Agatha said. 'You'd have felt compelled to defend my honour and reputation. You must never do that with Wilkes again. I am perfectly capable of looking after myself when it comes to his sort, but . . .' she leaned over and kissed him, '. . . I love you for it.'

'I'll drive you home,' he said, with a gentle smile. 'Wait here and I'll get my things.'

She watched him leave the room, and as the door swung closed, she felt like a dinner gong had just bonged in her chest – no, not a gong, an alarm bell, a klaxon! Had she just said 'love'? That wasn't a word that slipped out very often. Had she just told John that she loved him? No, surely not. Not directly, at least. It was just a mention in passing, not an actual declaration. That was different, wasn't it? Or was it? How did she *really* feel about him? She shook her head to clear her mind. This was some-thing she needed to think through carefully and she needed to think it through alone, probably with the help of a glass or two of Primitivo. John might be driving her home, but he would understand if she didn't invite him in. She frowned and reached into her handbag for her compact and lipstick. She might not want to 'lure him into the bedroom' tonight, but a girl still had to look her best.

The following morning, Agatha woke to the sound of her radio alarm. She had slept fitfully and yawned, sitting on the edge of her bed, struggling to shake off the shackles of sleep. She had tried to sit down and get everything straight in her head the night before, but it had been very late and, after several phone calls to the hospital to check on Margaret, she had managed neither to open a bottle of wine nor to close the case on her feelings about John Glass before she had fallen asleep on the sofa. Now, however, she had a busy day ahead and she had to get herself energised. Coffee first today, she thought, then a shower. Boswell and Hodge were delighted to scamper downstairs ahead of her for an early breakfast.

Agatha's first port of call was the all-too-familiar reception desk at Mircester General Hospital. While parking the car, she had seen Alf Bloxby leaving, so she knew the coast was clear for her to visit Margaret. She was given directions to the ward where Margaret was in a side room and was intercepted by a young female nurse on arrival.

'How is Mrs Bloxby doing?' Agatha asked. 'Can I see her?'

'She's been through a great deal with the operation last night,' the nurse explained, 'but she's strong and there have been no complications. She's had some sleep but was awake when I checked on her a few minutes ago. If she has gone back to sleep, please don't wake her and don't stay too long.'

'I won't,' Agatha promised, and opened the door to the room where Margaret lay in a bed that seemed far too large for her, tubes and wires linking her to drips and monitors. Agatha was relieved to see that there was no sign of the arrow, removed by the surgeon during the operation. At the sound of the door closing, Margaret turned her head towards Agatha.

'Good morning, Mrs Bloxby,' Agatha said, forcing a smile even as a tear rolled down her cheek.

'Good morning, Mrs Raisin,' Margaret greeted her, returning the smile. 'I'm afraid I can't offer you a glass of sherry today.'

'It's a bit early,' Agatha said with a little laugh, taking a seat at the bedside. 'Oh, Margaret, I'm so sorry! This is all my fault! I thought you were dead, just like Sir Godfrey! If it hadn't been for me, you would never . . .'

'Shush now, Agatha.' Margaret reached out to take her hand. 'You're not to blame. I was just in the wrong place at the wrong time. Had I been standing just one pace to the left, the thing would have missed me altogether.'

'And had you been standing a few inches to the right . . .'

'But I wasn't, was I? Now, about that prayer you said last night . . .'

They chatted for a few minutes more, until Margaret began to feel sleepy and Agatha left her to rest, promising to be back again as soon as she could. She paused for a moment outside Margaret's room, composed herself, then set off to find Roy Silver.

She was pleased to find Roy sitting up in bed, the swelling on his face much reduced, although the dark colours in the bruising, like a patch of oil on the pavement, were stronger than ever.

'What on earth have you been up to now, sweetie?' he greeted her. 'A graveyard in the middle of the night?'

'How do you know . . .?'

'It's all over the hospital!' Roy cried, with obvious delight. 'It's not every day they bring in someone who's been shot with an arrow, after all. Absolutely everyone's talking about it! How is Mrs Bloxby? They said she'd be okay.'

'She seems to be doing well.'

'Toni came in to see me on her way to work. She heard about last night from Bill Wong. The poor thing feels terribly guilty that she wasn't there with you in the graveyard. Thinks she could have made a difference.'

'Maybe. On the other hand, she might just have become another casualty.'

'As might you, sweetie! You really must take more care. I don't want anything happening to you.'

'Don't worry, Roy. I can look after myself. So . . . how are you feeling?'

Roy explained that he expected to be out of hospital at the weekend and they talked about what they might do while he stayed with her, although he ruled out riding for a while. Then she left to make her final visit, this time in the maternity wing.

Agatha found the maternity area surprisingly calm, almost tranquil. In her mind, she had imagined it to be a place of utter pandemonium, with constant shrieking and crying, and smelly little blanket bundles crawling everywhere like some kind of infestation. There was an occasional yelp, wail or gurgle but, on the whole, she found it a rather relaxed atmosphere. The least relaxed thing about the place was the young man standing in front of her, Spider, wearing a pristine white shirt, a jacket, clean jeans and a nervous expression.

'Mrs Raisin!' he said, with a huge grin. 'Come over here. I'll show you Amy and Grayson. They're both sound asleep right now.'

He led Agatha to a nearby bed where Amy was sleeping peacefully, and alongside her there was a transparent plastic cot. He held a finger to her lips to let her know she should be quiet and they leaned over the cot to look in. A small, wrinkled face and a tiny hand were visible above the blue blanket. Grayson, Agatha thought, looked sort of cute, but nowhere near as adorable as either of her cats. Still grinning, Spider led her away again.

'Brilliant, ain't he?' he said.

'Grayson looks lovely, Spider,' Agatha said, with as much conviction as she could muster.

'Thanks for the flowers and stuff,' he said. 'Arrived just in time. They'll be coming home today. Can't wait.'

'A quick question,' Agatha said. 'Can you remember who at the Archers used to call the targets Graysons?'

'That would be the Prides mainly,' Spider said, checking his watch. 'Must dash now, though. Got a job interview at a warehouse.'

'Good luck,' she called, watching him hurry off down the corridor, and a baby immediately let out an ear-piercing banshee howl. She left before it could set off a chain reaction.

By the time she walked into the office, Toni was the only one at her desk.

'Agatha!' she said, getting up and rushing over. 'Is Mrs Bloxby okay? Are you okay? Come in and sit down.'

'Mrs Bloxby is going to be fine,' Agatha said, 'and there's nothing wrong with me. I'm not the one who was shot with an arrow. We need to find those bastards, Toni!'

'Yes, of course,' Toni agreed. 'I'll do anything I can to help and . . . about yesterday lunchtime . . .'

'Oh, for goodness' sake don't go apologising,' Agatha said. 'If you say sorry, then I'll have to say sorry and we'll spend the rest of our lives saying sorry every time one of us says something stupid. We know each other too well for all that nonsense.'

'Okay,' Toni said, happy to hear the Agatha she knew back on song, 'but you must be exhausted.'

'I admit I didn't really get much sleep,' Agatha said, 'so I'm going to head home shortly. I've got a meeting this evening with Freddy Evans.'

'I should come, too,' Toni volunteered. 'You can't walk into another mess without someone to back you up.'

'Don't worry, I've got all the bases covered on this one,' Agatha said, 'but I need you to chase up the people at the lab and make sure we get that report through.'

206

She listed another few things that would keep Toni busy for a couple of hours, then, feeling suddenly weary, she left the office to head home.

Agatha checked herself in the mirror. The black skirt she was wearing was shorter than she might normally want, but she had the legs for it. She'd always thought her legs were her best feature – not as long as Alice's or Toni's but shapely, especially in the sheer black tights and black high heels. Just as the skirt was shorter, the heels were a little higher than she preferred. Roy had said Evans was quite short, so they would make her stand way taller than him. That might not bother him too much – most people he met were taller than him, after all – but Agatha felt they gave her a more powerful presence and, whatever Evans thought, a certain psychological advantage. The dark red blouse wasn't what she would have chosen for a business meeting and, overall, she thought the look was unsophisticated, cheap and flirty – pretty much perfect for impressing a man like Freddy Evans.

Half an hour later, she was sitting at a table in the Red Lion by the window, looking out over Carsely High Street. It was a dull evening, but the light of the day still lingered enough for her to see as far as the surrounding buildings allowed to the left and right. There were very few cars parked nearby, leaving ample space for the black Jaguar when it slowed to a halt outside the pub.

A heavily built man in his thirties with close-cropped hair, wearing a black suit over a black T-shirt, got out of the driver's side. He stood looking up and down the street, checking for anything out of the ordinary, the car door wide open and the engine running. Then he leaned forward, nodded to his passenger switched off the engine and closed the door.

Freddy Evans stepped out onto the pavement. He was a good twenty years older than his driver and far smaller, with short, dark hair greying at the sides. Agatha decided he was far too old to wear a blue business suit with a white collarless shirt and white tennis shoes. Surely it was a style for a younger man. No, she decided, it wasn't a style at all. He looked like a man who'd lost his shoes and was wearing a shirt he'd inherited from his grandfather. Yet, even from this distance, there was no escaping the cold darkness of his mean, narrow eyes. She pushed back her chair and went to greet the two men.

'Good evening, gentlemen,' she said, switching on her most dazzling professional smile. 'I'm glad you could make it.' She reached out to shake hands with Evans. He studied her for a moment, expressionless, then accepted her handshake without enthusiasm. Agatha decided that offering to shake hands with Evans's driver, who was scanning the pub just as he had done the street, was a wasted gesture.

'I have a table for us a little further round,' Agatha said, pushing the straps of her handbag higher up her forearm. 'It's just this way.'

Evans stared at the few regulars standing at the bar. Some had looked up when the two newcomers had walked in, but none made eye contact, swiftly returning to their beer and bar chat. There were no women in the pub, the only other customers a handful of men sitting at tables, reading the evening newspaper or tucking into the pub food. Agatha led them to a table by a side window. Evans pointed to one a few feet away, in the shadows.

'Not there,' he said, taking a seat with his back to the wall. 'We'll sit here.'

'Very well,' Agatha said, still smiling, watching the driver heave his bulk into the seat next to Evans. 'What can I get you?' She lowered her voice. 'I don't recommend eating here, but, for a rustic village pub, they do a very nice Burgundy.'

'Fine,' said Evans, 'but lemonade for Danny. He don't drink.'

'He don't . . . I mean doesn't . . . say much, either, does he?' Agatha said with a little laugh.

Both men stared at her, stony faced.

'I'll get the wine,' she said, hurrying to the bar.

Moments later, she returned with the bottle of Burgundy, the barman following with two wine glasses and a glass of lemonade. Agatha took her seat and poured the wine.

'Well, cheers!' she said, holding out her glass. Evans conceded a small clink, his eyes never leaving her face. 'Now, down to business,' she added, taking her phone, an envelope, a notepad and a pen from her handbag. She placed them neatly to one side, carefully laying the phone straight. 'It's new,' she said, sounding proud. 'I dropped the old one – smashed it to bits. Disaster. It's so much hassle transferring all your contacts and everything onto a new phone, isn't it?'

'Gerald Pride,' said Evans. 'When did he contact you?'

'Actually, he didn't,' Agatha said, allowing her smile to fade and fixing Evans with her bear-like eyes. 'I got in touch with him.'

'That ain't what you told me on the phone.'

'A detail,' Agatha said, her voice now low and steady as she adopted the persona of a hard-nosed businesswoman. 'I've spoken to him and I can get you the deal you want.'

'I heard he had his own plan.'

'He will be dropping his own plan and going with us.'

'What makes you so sure?'

'Because if he doesn't, I can make sure that he loses everything.'

'Is that so?' The hint of a sceptical smile creased the corner of Evans's mouth and he gave a slight shake of his head. 'How you goin' to do that then?'

Agatha opened the envelope and spread four photographs on the table.

'These are photographs of Gerald Pride with his mistress. His wife, Stephanie Pride, is the niece of Andrew Harkness, the senior partner in Pride & Harkness, despite their billing in the firm's name. If Stephanie ever sees these photos, she will have her uncle kick Pride out of the firm. At the moment, she lives with Pride in a house that she inherited from her parents. Uncle Andrew will make sure she keeps that. The divorce will cost Pride his business, his home and most of whatever he stands to gain from Sir Godfrey's estate.

'If, on the other hand, he plays ball with us, Stephanie need never see the photos, there will be no divorce and we all earn a tidy sum.'

'I had my doubts about you,' Evans said, sitting back and folding his arms, a thin smile on his lips. 'So I asked around. Word came back that you're a tough cookie who usually gets what she wants. Now I can see how you got that reputation. You're not scared to play dirty. I think we might be able to do business together.'

'I'm glad you went to the trouble of checking up on me, Mr Evans. I respect that sort of thoroughness. It's always good to know who you're dealing with. So I know you'll understand why I thought it would be a good idea for me to find out a bit about you, too. You have quite a reputation.'

'Believe me, Mrs Raisin, my reputation gets me respect. People I deal with know I'm not a man to be crossed.'

'Oh, I believe you all right,' Agatha said, gathering the photographs and slotting them back in the envelope. 'That's why I've put all my cards on the table. I want you to know how I'm going to play this game before we get into it. There's a lot of money to be made here, but I don't want to end up like Roy Silver.'

'Silver was an idiot, he made promises he couldn't keep. He let me down bad. It don't pay to take the piss with me, Mrs Raisin.'

'I wouldn't dream of it, Mr Evans. I'm guessing that you dumped Roy outside my office because you knew I'd help spread the word about what happens when you disappoint Freddy Evans.'

'Silver got what was comin' to him,' Evans said, shrugging. 'You'll get the same if you don't play your cards right.'

211

'I'm not frightened of a little man like you,' Agatha taunted him, 'and I'm not scared of big Danny boy, either.'

'Well, you should be!' Evans snarled. 'One word from me and Danny will give you a taste of the beating we gave your pal Silver, only he's not so gentle with the ladies!'

'I'm sure he's not a gentle man in any sense of the term,' Agatha said, then spoke directly at her phone. 'I think I've got all I need from this meeting. What do you say, boys?'

John Glass appeared at the table from one direction, Bill Wong from the other.

'I think you got more than enough, Mrs Raisin,' John said, presenting his police warrant card. Evans gave Agatha a look of absolute fury.

'Oh dear.' Agatha feigned realisation with raised eyebrows. 'My new phone – I must have left my call to Inspector Glass connected the whole time. He heard everything.'

Evans lunged across the table at her and she stood up, stepping back and knocking over her chair. At the same time, Danny reached into his jacket, drawing out a dark, glinting wooden baton. He swung it at John, who dodged aside, the two standing and facing off.

'Well, well!' John said. 'A police truncheon. I haven't seen one of those in thirty years.'

Danny swung again and John swayed backwards, avoiding the blow and holding up a small spray canister. He sent a jet of liquid into Danny's eyes. The big man screamed in pain and collapsed on the ground, the truncheon falling from his hand, rolling across the floor.

Meanwhile, Evans was struggling with Bill Wong. Bill stumbled on Agatha's chair and Evans squirmed free, stepping forward to run for the door only for Agatha to raise her knee and drive the tip of her heel through the top of his tennis shoe. He fell forward, squealing, 'You broke my foot, you bitch!' and clutching his bloodied tennis shoe. Agatha snatched the truncheon from the floor, raising it to shoulder height and taking aim at his face. A strong hand gripped her wrist.

'We use reasonable force, Agatha,' Bill Wong said quietly. 'Reasonable force only – otherwise we're as bad as them.'

He stooped to slap his handcuffs on Evans just as John was doing the same to Danny.

'Hurts like hell, doesn't it, Danny?' he said. 'You're blind now, as well, but unlike Roy Evans, in a couple of hours you'll be okay. It's one of the new things we use nowadays – PAVA spray. Much more effective than the old truncheon.'

Two uniformed officers arrived from the pub's kitchen area to haul Danny upright while another two did the same for Evans. Pulling on a latex glove, Bill took the truncheon from Agatha, slipping it into an evidence bag.

'Do you think that animal used that thing on Roy?' Agatha asked.

'Could be,' Bill replied. 'Forensics are bound to be able to tell us.' Then, turning to the officers escorting the two prisoners to the front door, he added, 'They'll both need medical attention once they're safely in custody.'

Passing the bar, Agatha was hailed by Bert Simpson, husband to Doris, her cleaning lady.

'By heck, Mrs Raisin,' Bert said, his cronies gathered round, 'that were the most exciting thing to happen in the Red Lion since you told us all you'd be parading around your garden naked whenever you felt like it.'

'I aim to please, Bert.' Agatha gave them a wink and walked out into the street.

John and Bill were watching Evans and Danny being loaded into the back of a police van while two young constables debated which of them should drive the Jag to the station.

'This must be the car they used to abduct Roy,' Agatha said. 'They would have bundled him into the boot. We might find bloodstains there, or hairs. Solid evidence.'

'Forensics will go over it all,' Bill said.

'Pop it open anyway,' said John. 'We can have a quick look as long as we don't touch anything.'

One of the constables pressed a button on the key fob and the boot lid slowly opened automatically. Inside was a sea of blue-and-yellow Mircester United merchandise in transparent plastic bags.

'Isn't that what you were wearing the other day?' asked Bill.

'It is indeed,' Agatha agreed, smiling, thinking hard. 'Evans's son-in-law is a director of Mircester United. This is how they were getting the fake gear into the stadium. Danny must have driven his two VIP passengers into a private car park area. Nobody would search a car carrying a director of the club, after all. Then they simply distributed it to their lackeys who quietly flogged it off to the fans.'

'Is this a police matter?' John asked.

'I suppose it will be, if Mircester or any of the other clubs involved want to press charges,' Agatha said, then laughed. 'Patrick and Simon are going to be *so* cross with me for cracking their case before they did!'

'I'm sorry, Agatha,' John said, sounding truly apologetic, 'but we need to go back to the station yet again.'

'Mircester Police Station and Mircester General Hospital,' Agatha said, with a sigh. 'I seem to spend more time there than I do at home!'

Chapter Ten

'Good morning, Mr Pride,' Agatha said, adopting a pleasant yet purposeful telephone voice. 'It's Agatha Raisin
here.'

'I have nothing to say to you,' Gerald Pride said,
gruffly. 'Please do not . . .'

'Don't hang up, Mr Pride. At the moment, you're in a
whole heap of trouble. This phone call could save your
bacon.'

'What are you talking about?'

'Do I have to catalogue your entire list of woes, Mr
Pride? It's all rather depressing, really. Still, here goes.
Top of the list is the one thing that you and I have in
common – we are both suspects in the murder of your
father.'

'That's preposterous! I did *not* murder my father!'

'I didn't do it either, Mr Pride, but there's a certain
senior police officer who would love to pin the murder on
me. He will, eventually, when he has an uncharacteristic
attack of common sense, have to focus his attention elsewhere, and that's when he'll start homing in on you.'

'Why would he do that?'

'Oh, come on, Mr Pride, you're a lawyer – you know how these things work. He'll look at who had most to gain from the old man's death, and that's probably you. Having established a motive, he'll then decide whether you had the opportunity. He'll see if he can place you in the woods at the time of your father's death.'

'He can't. I have a watertight alibi. I was at home with my wife.'

'And so far, Mr Pride – or would you rather I call you Gerald?'

'No, I would not.'

'Well, I'm going to call you Gerald, anyway. So far, Gerald, Stephanie has backed up your alibi, but what if she changes her story? What if she decides that, given the size of your lovely home in Lower Burlip and the fact that you're barely on speaking terms and unlikely to have spent much time in the same room, she can't be sure that you didn't sneak out of the house at some point?'

'Why would my wife do that?'

'Because she hates you, Gerald. She knows all about your affair with Petula and she's just about ready to feed you into the shredder. She'll go to the police, and she'll go to her uncle. With a murder investigation hanging over your head and his niece's divorce to oversee, Uncle Andrew will have you out the door quicker than you can say "philanderer".

'Can you see how that list of woes is adding up, Gerald? You'll have no job, your reputation will be in tatters, meaning that no one will want to hire you, you'll have no home because Stephanie and her uncle will hang on to

217

the house. You'll be under investigation by the police, and you'll still have all the problems associated with your father's estate to deal with – although you're not likely to see much benefit from that after Stephanie and Uncle Andrew get their claws into it.'

'What makes you think you can do anything about any of that?'

'I don't think I can, Gerald, I know I can. All I need you to do is help me organise a little get-together . . .'

Agatha guided her car along the rutted track, tutting when its underside scraped and crunched against the ground. She considered stopping to park as she had done on her previous visit to Carseworth Manor, then remembered that she had left her wellies by her kitchen door, waiting to have the mud hosed off them. She was wearing the dark green skirt and jacket again, and had matched them with a pair of green shoes that weren't too high for walking but would never cope with this track – and they were suede. The car would just have to suffer.

'What's this all about, Mrs Raisin?' asked Petula, her passenger.

'What I'm hoping it will be is a resolution,' Agatha replied, wrestling with the steering wheel. 'A chance for everyone involved to start getting on with the rest of their lives.'

The track levelled out and widened when they reached the house, where two cars were parked by the front steps. Gerald Pride's was one of them, Benny Lambert's ancient

Land Rover was the other. Petula stared at them, clearly recognising both vehicles.

'I told you it was to be a family gathering,' Agatha said. 'You may not be family, exactly, but I very much doubt if you'll want to miss out.'

They walked into the house and, hearing voices from a set of double doors to the right, they made their way into the drawing room. There was silence as they entered, all eyes on them. Elizabeth was lolling on a threadbare sofa, Benny sitting in an armchair beside her. Gerald stood by an ornate, if rather soot-stained, stone fireplace, leaning an elbow on the mantelpiece, and Stephanie was pacing back and forth by the French windows.

'What's *she* doing here?' Stephanie spat, narrowing her eyes at Petula.

'I will explain everything in just a moment,' Agatha said. 'Please be patient. It will be worth hearing.'

'The kitchen's just through there,' Petula said, pointing to a door on the far side of the fireplace. 'Maybe I could make us all some tea?'

'Ha!' Elizabeth crowed. 'Knows her place, doesn't she?'

'You're not a servant in this house any longer, Petula,' said Gerald.

'Nevertheless,' Agatha said, 'it's very kind of you to offer, Petula. Tea is a great idea.'

There was silence when Petula left and Agatha made no attempt to break it. She looked around the large room, taking in the tired décor, the dusty surfaces and the shabby rugs covering ramshackle floorboards. In places, attempts had been made to clean or tidy. Some of the pictures hanging around the wall had been dusted and in one corner stood a collection of packing cases that someone had been filling with ornaments, oddities and nick-nacks. Agatha spotted an implement by the fireplace that aroused her curiosity. It was a closed copper pan about the size of a large dinner plate attached to a yard-long wooden handle.

'This is unusual,' she said, looking to Gerald. 'What is it?'

'It's a bedpan,' he said, as though humouring her. 'A warming pan. A servant would put embers from the fire in the pan, then carry it upstairs to slip it into your bed to warm it.'

'Some of the servants knew far better ways to warm your bed,' Stephanie scoffed.

Any further comments were curtailed by the sound of footsteps in the hall and the appearance of Toni, accompanied by Spider.

'Ah, Toni, welcome!' Agatha greeted her. 'And you, too, Mr Hendricks. How are Amy and the baby?'

'They're doin' great, Mrs Raisin,' Spider answered. 'They're both at home. Will this take long? Only I want to stop by and see them before I go to work.'

'You got the job! Congratulations!' Agatha applauded him.

'Trial period,' Spider said. 'Don't want to be late.'

'We'll get you out of here in plenty of time, Spider, don't worry,' Agatha assured him.

'We're not all here to celebrate this numbskull getting a job, are we?' Elizabeth sneered.

220

'No, we're not, Elizabeth,' Agatha said, ignoring the cruel taunt in Elizabeth's voice and turning to see Petula appear carrying a fully laden tea tray. 'But now we are all here, we can get started.'

Petula put the tea tray on a low table and proceeded to pour a cup for everyone. Agatha took her cup and saucer over to the door, standing where she could see the assembled group, and be seen by all of them.

'The thing that's brought us all together here is not Spider getting a job, however important a fresh start that is for him and his new family, but the murder of Sir Godfrey Pride. The death of Sir Godfrey has affected us all, not least me, given that I was the one who was with him when he died.'

She looked around the room. Toni had taken a seat near the door. Spider was standing behind the sofa. Everyone was watching her. She had their full attention.

'All of us became suspects in the murder investigation, apart from Toni, of course. The only suspect I could rule out at first was myself, because I know for an absolute fact that I didn't do it . . .'

'Well, I didn't . . .' Gerald started to interrupt but Agatha silenced him with a wave of her hand.

'You were the prime suspect, Gerald,' she continued. 'On the face of it, you had the most to gain from your father's death. You were at odds with him over the plans to redevelop this place, you wanted to take back the land that the Prides had previously given to the church, and you were fighting with him about a new will that wasn't to his liking.

'On top of all that, your wife, Stephanie, was clearly heard vowing to kill Sir Godfrey. The two of you, working together, had plenty of motive and, providing each other with alibis, plenty of opportunity.

'You may have been working together, but there's also the possibility that you were working instead with someone else, Gerald. For some time now it would seem that your marriage hasn't been working and you have slipped back into the arms of your former love – Petula.'

Petula looked startled and Gerald shifted uncomfortably, but only Spider looked surprised.

'It seems that everyone here knew about the affair except you, Spider. Yet you, Petula, knew all about Spider. When I asked you, you flatly denied that Sir Godfrey could have been either Spider's father or the father of Amy's baby. Why sound so certain, especially after you made a point of telling me all about Spider's mother, and Spider, and Amy? Simple – you wanted to get me interested in them. The note in Sir Godfrey's pocket, luring him into the woods, was signed "A", after all, "A" for Amy, as was the note luring me into the graveyard.

'But what you really wanted me to find out, Petula, was that Spider and Amy were trying to get money out of Sir Godfrey by telling him that Amy's baby was his. They were relying on him being so befuddled with age and years of drinking that he would pay out to keep things quiet.

'Petula hoped that would make you my number one suspect, Spider, and she had a point. When threatening to disgrace the old man didn't work, your and Amy's next step would be threats of violence, and then, when it became clear that he had no money to give you, perhaps the situation got out of control and you killed him in a fit of anger. The murder weapon was, after all, something with which you were very familiar – an arrow.

'Then again, you were all familiar with arrows, weren't you? You have all been involved with the Ancombe Archers to a greater or lesser degree. You are, Elizabeth, and Benny. Petula, of course, was there at the fete and has a reasonable alibi in that she was with the archers. Spider's alibi is much the same, although it's possible that either of you could have sneaked off for a few minutes. Maybe Spider had a recurrence of his nose bleed. That's been a problem of late, hasn't it, Spider?

'I'm told, Elizabeth, that you claim you were at home with Benny in Comfrey Magna, but you and he only have each other to confirm that so, like your brother and Stephanie, you don't have the strongest of alibis. You also have a very particular motive for murdering your father – revenge. He didn't like Benny and he didn't like you being with him, so he dropped you from his will, or did he? I think there's been a bit of will juggling going on of late and you, or possibly Gerald, may have persuaded Sir Godfrey to reinstate you. That makes little difference, however, because it simply moves your motive on from revenge to profit. You don't have a job and Benny drifts from one to another, so life is a real struggle for you financially. Things could be so much different with an injection of cash from your father's estate.

'So much for the suspects and their motives, now let's consider the murder scene. First there's the arrow. You all know how deadly an arrow can be and it was no accident or moment of convenience that led to the arrow being the weapon of choice. The murderers, you see, wanted to create confusion. At first, as the police thought, it might have been seen as an accident, Sir Godfrey having been shot during the archery demonstration.

'We now know that he wasn't shot, but stabbed with the arrow. That meant someone had to get up close. Who can get closer to a man than his lover? When Sir Godfrey was found with his trousers round his ankles, it would be fair to assume that some sort of sexual encounter had taken place. I'm afraid that, and the note, and your claims that Grayson was Sir Godfrey's child, point to you and Amy being the murderers, Spider.'

'No!' Spider cried. 'We didn't do it! I swear we didn't!'

'No, I don't think you did, Spider, but the baby and Sir Godfrey—'

Agatha was interrupted by footsteps in the hall, Simon appearing at the door and handing a document to Toni. Toni then took it to Agatha.

'Baby and Sir Godfrey nothing!' roared Gerald. 'A simple DNA test will show my father had nothing to do with that child!'

'Simon and Patrick are outside if you need them,' Toni whispered. Agatha nodded.

'A simple DNA test will do nothing of the sort.' Agatha stared at Gerald. 'A DNA test will show that they *are* related, but you know that already, don't you? Comparing baby Grayson's DNA with that of your father would show a very close relationship. That was what you

thought would be the final nail in Spider's coffin . . .
wasn't it, Elizabeth?'

'I haven't a clue what you're talking about.' Elizabeth
dismissed Agatha with a flick of her wrist.

'Oh, but you do. You've been listening very carefully,
just like you listen to your brother. You may not be the
closest of siblings but you do talk. You must have been
delighted when Gerald told you that your father wanted
you back in the will, but not so pleased when he told you
that there was to be a third beneficiary. You'd have to
share your inheritance.

'Your father refused to sign the will Gerald had drawn
up because he wanted to include someone else, and now
I know who. The report just handed to me is an analysis
of two DNA samples. They're not from Sir Godfrey and
baby Grayson. They're from Gerald and Spider. We used
your hair, Gerald, and blood from your nose, Spider. The
tests show beyond a shadow of a doubt that you share
the same father. Spider, Gerald is your half-brother. Sir
Godfrey was your father.'

'Really?' Spider's mouth dropped open.

'When Sir Godfrey told you about Spider, Gerald,'
Agatha continued, 'maybe feeling guilty after all these
years, or maybe, knowing that Amy was expecting, feeling he should provide for the grandchild that neither you
nor Elizabeth had produced, you must have been furious.
Yet he must also have told you that Spider was asking
him for money anyway. He probably thought that was
quite funny in an ironic sort of way, but I bet you were
livid.

'When you told Elizabeth, I'm guessing she hit the roof. How did it feel, Elizabeth, finding out you had a half-brother? How did it feel, having just got back into the will, to discover that you were now having to give part of your inheritance to Spider? Insufferable, no doubt. So you began plotting.

'You and Gerald called the archery targets Graysons because they had arrows shot into them just like your ancestor, Grayson Pride, when he was killed by his lover. That story was your inspiration. You set the whole thing up to make it look like Sir Godfrey was also killed by his lover, with your fictional lover perhaps trying to disguise the killing as an accident.

'You knew that Spider was trying to extort money from Sir Godfrey. You also knew that would come out during the murder investigation. Then, when Sir Godfrey's DNA was compared to baby Grayson's, you thought there would be a close enough match for everyone to believe the lie that Spider was telling the old man. A grandson, after all, carries a hefty dose of his grandfather's DNA. Even if it wasn't enough for the experts to believe Sir Godfrey was the father, the family tie would be obvious. Any investigator would then want to test Spider and the results would show him to be Sir Godfrey's son. That was all to the good, because it made the old man's neglect of him over the years even more of a motive for murder.

'So you planned the murder as a way of getting rid of your father and blaming it all on your half-brother. You took your father for a walk in the woods, the wayward daughter reunited with her old dad, then you killed him, dropped his trousers and left him there to die – or rather, you had your accomplice stab him, because when Sir Godfrey was dying in my arms he tried to tell me something. I thought he was calling me a "filly" like he had earlier that morning, but he was actually trying to tell me who murdered him – Philip. Philip Benjamin Lambert.

'Elizabeth distracted him, then held him steady, didn't she, Benny? Then you stabbed the arrow into his chest just like she told you to! Then, when you thought I might be closing in on you, Elizabeth, you lured me to the graveyard and an innocent woman – the most innocent in the world – almost lost her life!'

Gerald collapsed into an armchair with a groan of misery. Agatha looked towards him and, seeing she was distracted, Elizabeth sprinted for the kitchen, closely followed by Benny. Agatha charged after them only to have the door slammed in her face. She wrenched it open, stepping into the kitchen to see Elizabeth scrabbling in a tall metal cupboard. Inside she could see a couple of modern bows, a stock of arrows and, to her horror, a shotgun that Elizabeth handed to Benny. He levelled it directly at Agatha. She pulled the door closed behind her. The last thing she wanted was Toni to come charging in and end up like Margaret.

'A shotgun, Benny?' Agatha swallowed hard, her mouth dry. 'More effective than a bow in here, I guess.'

She looked around the kitchen which, she decided, was actually more of a pantry with a low ceiling, a few storage cupboards and a sink. Benny moved slowly to cover the open door leading to the corridor without ever taking his aim from Agatha. The only other door, save for the one behind Agatha, led out to the garden.

'I'll shoot you if I has to, Mrs Raisin,' Benny said. 'Don't make me shoot you.'

'Do it, Benny!' Elizabeth yelled. 'Then we go this way!' She moved towards the garden door.

'I . . . don't want to . . .' Benny said. 'We done too much, Liz. Where will we run to? We ain't got no cash. They'll track us down. Then it's prison . . .'

'No, Benny,' Elizabeth said, softly. 'We can get away. We can start again far away, and . . .'

'That ain't right, Liz. It'll be prison for us. I won't never see you again. I won't never be able to look after you no more. This here's the end of the line for us.'

'Listen to me, Benny,' Agatha appealed to him. 'You've done some bad things, but you mustn't make it worse. You're not a bad person at heart.'

'We're bad people,' Benny said, turning to face Elizabeth. 'No doubt about it. So we'll go now, Liz. Together. First you . . .' he pointed the gun at her, '. . . then me.' He swivelled the gun for an instant to show how he'd take the second shot under the chin.

Suddenly there was a roar like a charging lioness and Toni appeared in the hall doorway, swinging the warming pan like a battle axe. It connected with the back of Benny's head with a clang like a cracked cymbal, the noise then completely obliterated by the explosion of the shotgun firing. In the enclosed space the shotgun blast, pointed straight at the ancient ceiling, was utterly deafening. The gun smoke in the air was immediately overwhelmed by a cloud of plaster dust. A splintering crack announced the collapse of the ceiling, which seemed to tear itself apart, wooden beams, dust and plaster debris raining down on them. Agatha staggered back against the door, blinded by the cloud of dust, coughing and shutting her eyes tight.

When she opened them a moment later, the dust was settling on a scene of utter mayhem, with white-crusted figures struggling on the floor. Simon was sitting on top of a disoriented Benny, pinning his arms. Patrick was unloading the shotgun and Toni was struggling with Elizabeth. Agatha stepped towards them and Elizabeth flung Toni aside before taking a swipe at Agatha, who caught her wrist, swinging her against the sink.

'Snakes and bastards!' she hissed. 'Margaret nearly died because of you!' Then she landed a right hook to Elizabeth's jaw, sending her spinning to the floor, where she cowered, whimpering.

With her staff subduing Benny and Elizabeth in the kitchen, a dishevelled, dust-covered Agatha marched back into the drawing room.

'You better all stay right where you are,' she growled, glowering from beneath a furrowed brow. 'The police will be here shortly. Make a move before then and you'll have me to deal with.'

As she promised, police officers were quickly on the scene, Agatha detailing what had happened to a uniformed sergeant she vaguely knew. She then sat down with an utterly baffled Spider, trying to explain that he and Amy were in the clear, although the police would want to talk to him about his attempt to swindle Sir Godfrey. He then phoned Amy to check in with her and Agatha promised to phone the warehouse to let them know Spider was going to be late, entertaining the manager so much with the story of the afternoon that he said Spider should take some time out and start work on Monday.

Alice Wong walked into the room, took a look around and immediately spotted Agatha.

'Agatha,' she said, hurrying up, 'are you all right?'

'Just a little plastered,' Agatha sighed, plucking a chunk of kitchen ceiling out of her hair. 'I know that's an old joke, but right now I need a bit of cheer. Seems like every time I come to Carseworth, I get covered in muck.'

'Well, well, it's Constable Alice.' Stephanie strolled towards them, having managed to provide herself with a glass of white wine.

'Hello, Stephanie,' Alice smiled.

'You two clearly know each other,' Agatha observed.

'We grew up in the same street,' Alice explained. 'My parents live just a few houses away from Stephanie. We went to the same school, but . . .'

'Go on, say it!' Stephanie laughed. 'I'm a good deal older than young Alice, here. I used to be quite jealous of her, knowing that she'd always be younger, always be prettier than me, but I . . .' She paused, her head cocked slightly to one side, studying Alice's face. 'How are you feeling?'

'I'm . . . great,' Alice said, shrugging nervously.

'What do you mean?' Agatha asked. 'Why did you ask how she was feeling?'

'Oh, come on, Mrs Raisin,' Stephanie grinned. 'You're the great detective, after all. You played a very skilful game this afternoon – not quite the game I was expecting, but it's a result I can work with. Gerald must have known what Elizabeth was plotting. Uncle Andrew will wipe the floor with him, so I've an entertaining few months to look forward to. So, it would seem, does Alice. Take a look at her. Use your detective observation skills, or whatever you call them.'

'Alice, what . . .?' Agatha gave a confused frown.

'I'm pregnant,' Alice said, beaming with excitement. 'Bill and I are having a baby!'

'A baby?' Agatha gasped. 'You two didn't waste much time, did you? I mean, the wedding was only . . . I, um . . . congratulations!'

'Thank you, Agatha.' Alice gave her a hug then pulled back, brushing transferred plaster dust off her jacket.

'Never worked for me and Gerald,' Stephanie said with a hint of regret, 'but then nothing ever did, really. You look after yourself, young lady.'

Stephanie wandered off, leaving Agatha to quiz Alice.

'So what will happen to your job?' she asked. 'Will they sack you?'

'Sack me? Of course not,' Alice replied. 'I'll have leave when the baby is due and then I'll go back to work. I love working with the police, but I might not want to go back as a detective. I'm sure I'll be able to find a different role, maybe part-time, maybe . . . oh, I don't know!' She laughed. 'I keep thinking about the baby and I get excited and a bit scared and I don't know whether I'm coming or going!'

'You'll be fine, Alice. I'm really happy for you and Bill. Now, do we have to do statements and suchlike?'

'I'm afraid so,' Alice agreed, leading Agatha over to a side table where there were two convenient chairs. 'I think your outfit might be ruined,' she sympathised.

'Not to worry,' said Agatha. 'It was never really a favourite.'

Bill turned up a little later and there was another awkward hug and more happy congratulations before he, having been briefed by Agatha, sat down for a serious chat with Spider, issuing a stern warning and telling him to keep his nose clean in future. Agatha saw that as wise advice, especially given the trouble Spider had with his nose. She then took a phone call from a very concerned John. Detective Chief Inspector Wilkes, on the other hand, was conspicuous by his absence. While Agatha would have delighted in rubbing his nose in his own ignominy at her having cracked the Pride murder case, she was equally glad not to see him at all. By the time she arrived home that evening, all she wanted to do was bin her clothes and stand under a hot shower.

*   *   *

She had dried her hair and was applying a little light make-up when her doorbell rang. Shrugging on a robe, she trotted downstairs and spied James through the peep-hole in her front door.

'Thought you might like some company,' he said. 'I heard what's been going on and, well, I want to say sorry for being such an arse. You're right. You're absolutely right that there's no going back and we can't expect to be able to rekindle old flames to try to manufacture a relationship that doesn't really exist any more.'

'James, I . . .'

'No, just let me finish. It took me ages to work out how I would say all this, so I don't want to lose the plot now. You were right in saying what you did, but I know I was right to a degree as well. Life really is too short to waste on negative emotions. Going forward, we will be happiest as ex-husband and wife, happiest as the best of neighbours and happiest as the closest of friends. We owe it to each other to always be there for each other. That's what I want and I think that's what you want, too, so I brought this as a kind of . . . peace offering.'

He held up a bottle of wine and two glasses.

'James,' she said, 'you're an angel.' She put her arms round his neck and kissed him. 'You'd best come in while I get dressed and . . .'

Looking over his shoulder, she could see a car driving off along Lilac Lane. She recognised it immediately.

'Ah . . . that was John's car,' she said slowly.

'John? Oh, I see,' James nodded, holding up the glasses and wine, 'and he saw this, and us. Were I him, I'd be feeling a bit confused and upset right now.'

'I'm afraid he might be,' Agatha said with a worried expression.

'Well, our peace pact can wait,' James said, hefting the bottle in his hand and turning towards the low fence. 'You'd best go after him and explain.'

'Thank you, James. I think I best had.'

She found him in his dance studio, sitting in a deckchair in the middle of the floor, listening to big band music. If Agatha had to hazard a guess, she'd have said it was Benny Goodman. By John's chair was a side table on which sat a bottle of wine and a single glass, half full – or maybe, Agatha thought, judging by the deflated appearance of the figure slumped in the chair, the glass was half empty.

He looked up as she stepped onto the floor and smiled at her. The smile was overflowing with affection but was, at the same time, the resigned smile of a man who had conceded defeat. He used a small remote control to turn Benny Goodman's volume down to a background level.

'I saw you in Lilac Lane,' she said. There was no other chair in the room so, before he could struggle out of the deckchair, she knelt next to him and sat on her heels. Now they were at the same eye level and she felt she could talk to him without him suffering the disadvantage of being lower down.

'I saw you, too . . . with James.'

'I guessed,' she said, reaching for his glass to take a sip of his wine. 'Well, Mr Policeman, what did they teach you at detective school about jumping to conclusions – putting two and two together and making five?'

'Sometimes,' he said, retrieving his wine and taking a sip himself before placing it on the table, ready to be shared, 'seeing is believing.'

'Yet, no matter what you see, things aren't always what they seem,' she countered, helping herself to another sip.

'I'm sorry,' he said with a sigh. 'It's been a funny old day – a bit of a rollercoaster, you know? Ups and downs.'

'Wait a minute,' she said with a questioning frown. 'What's happened to your shift pattern? Shouldn't you be at work?'

'No, I should not,' he said. 'I am now an ex-police detective, retired with immediate effect.'

'What? They can't do that, can they? Is this Wilkes's doing? You can't—'

'Calm down, Agatha,' he said, gesturing for her to relax and smiling to show that all was well. 'I was aiming to retire in a few weeks but I had another bust-up with Wilkes and he decided that our "personality clash" was not conducive to the smooth running of the department, so he's arranged for me to go early.'

'Really?' Agatha was sceptical. 'He's always complaining about how short-staffed he is.'

'He'll make sure there are a few key promotions, then split some responsibilities to take up the slack. My retirement will probably be good news for Bill Wong.'

'So is retirement an "up" or a "down"?' She took another sip of wine and offered the glass back to him.

'Sort of both at the same time,' he laughed, taking the glass, 'but seeing you with James was definitely a down.'

'Now you're being ridiculous.'

'Am I?' He drank some wine. 'How can I ever really hope to compete? He's your ex-husband who still lives right next door and you two seem as close as ever. You obviously care about him a lot.'

'I do – and that's why, after the health scare he's just had and all he and I have been through together, I'm hugely relieved that we've agreed to being friends. James and I both know in our hearts that we can never re-establish any kind of romantic relationship. We'd end up hating each other all over again, and neither of us wants that. We want to stay friends. He knows that I'm not in love with him.'

John straightened himself in the chair, looking far more alert, as though a shock of hope had surged through him at high voltage.

'Might you . . .' he said tentatively, '. . . maybe be a little in love with me?'

'I might,' she smiled, helping herself to more wine, 'but that remains to be seen.'

'I've a great idea about how you can find out!' he announced, leaning forward. 'I had been talking to some people about the possibility of a job when I retired and I called them earlier today to say that my retirement had been brought forward and they've got an urgent vacancy to fill. They want me to start next week!'

'How can I help you with a job?' she asked. 'I have my own business to run. What is this job anyway?'

'Teaching dance on a luxury cruise liner,' he said, enthusiasm lighting up his face. 'It's a chance to travel on a voyage that's going right around the world, teaching dance – which I love – and getting paid for it, too! Come with me, Agatha! We could do it all together!'

'Sounds like a dream job, but how long does this cruise take?'

'It visits all the most glamorous places you could think of around the Mediterranean, the United States, South America, the Far East, Australia – it takes a whole year!'

'A year?' Agatha's eyes widened. Not so long ago another lovely man, an engineer named Chris, had asked her to go away with him. He had wanted them to start a new life in California. She couldn't go with Chris and, with a heavy heart, she had to admit to herself that she couldn't go with John, either. 'That's a very long time. John, I have my business to run, people who rely on me, a whole life that I've built right here in the Cotswolds. I can't just disappear for an entire year at the drop of a hat.'

'I understand,' he said, sounding suddenly dejected. 'I always reckoned that would be the "down" from the cruise job's "up".'

'I'm sorry, John.' She pushed down on the floor with the palms of her hands and levered herself to her feet as elegantly as she could. 'Truly, I am, but that really wouldn't work.'

He said nothing and she walked towards the door. She had taken only three steps, however, when she turned back to face him.

'On the other hand,' she said, thoughts still tumbling through her mind, 'we could take a look at the cruise itinerary together. I could always jet out to catch up with you for a tango in Argentina . . .'

The shock of hope galvanised him once again and he jumped to his feet.

'Or a jive in New Jersey!' he offered, grinning.

'Or a polka in Acapulco!' she added.

'I'm not sure that Mexico's the right place for . . .' He made a pretence at confusion.

'Never mind!' she laughed. 'Mexico's not the right place and I can't polka but it sounded good! And the idea sounds good, too . . . doesn't it?'

'Like music to my ears,' he said, with what Agatha suspected was a tiny tear in the corner of the big, tough, ex-detective's eye. 'Would you care to have a little practice with me?'

He turned up the music and she stepped forward into his arms.

'I would love to,' she said.

And as they drifted off around the dancefloor, she thought of all the most romantic cities where they might rendezvous, all the most amazing places where they might dance, but right at that moment, she couldn't imagine anywhere in the world she would rather be than a suburban back garden in Mircester.